MALADY

Malady

A novel
by

NINA WILSON

BOOKS

Adelaide Books
New York/Lisbon
2019

MALADY
A novel
By Nina Wilson

Published by Adelaide Books, New York / Lisbon
adelaidebooks.org

Editor-in-Chief
Stevan V. Nikolic

For any information, please address Adelaide Books
at info@adelaidebooks.org

or write to:

Adelaide Books
244 Fifth Ave. Suite D27
New York, NY, 10001

ISBN-10: 1-949180-04-2
ISBN-13: 978-1-949180-04-6

Printed in the United States of America

Chapter One

1920

Amos Perry, a giant of a man, looked like an onion left out in the sun to dry. He paced before us one hand clutching a crude oak pulpit, his skin gaunt and stretched over thick, angular bone, and a long crow's neck trembling with his voice. His eyes were raging, his voice thunderous, and his fists were clenched so tightly I thought his nails would dig into his skin long enough that they'd bleed and he'd bear the marks of Christ. How one man could hold so much fury and energy one moment, and the next be lounging in the back sipping at some water, I didn't know. He was not an approachable man. Nor was he a man who aged. In the process of digging through my memory, I didn't remember our pastor looking any different than he did right at this moment. He wore the same thing every day, nothing but black to signify the grief of the dying world.

Mama sat beside me, her back straight as could be, her hands folded politely on her ironed skirt. Her face was hard and calm, beginning to wrinkle with age and stress. There were little lines around her eyes. I could hear her breathe, something was catching in her throat just slightly, making a clicking sound.

I'd rather listen to that than have Reverend Perry yelling at me, or watch the veins in his neck throb. Father wasn't any more interesting though. He smelled like soap. He always wanted to be clean when going into the house of God. His face was perfectly shaved. He looked strange amongst all the men here who were gruff, rough, and unkempt. They were men of the land with beards to match. Father owned the general store. The only land we worked was the garden at the back of our house.

I wanted to get back to the garden, but Reverend Perry's loud booming voice forced me to pay attention to his sermon. I'd stop being scared of his words in about six days, and by then I'd have to come back and be scared all over again at the wrath of God.

"You deserve you to know! You must know! The Great War is not over! No, it was but a battle! A taste of what is to come! For Matthew says, 'and you will hear of wars, and rumors of wars, see that you are not alarmed, for this must take place, but the end is not yet. For nation will rise against nation, and kingdom against kingdom, and there will be famines and there will be earthquakes!'" He shoved his fist into the air, my mother shoved her fist into my leg. I was slouching. "The war has changed us, it has changed our society, and our children. It awoke the young people of our world to pleasure seeking behavior, to the fear that they will not live to experience all that life has to offer. The war proved how shakable the world and the people in it are! They are not cynical, smug individuals.

"We as the Remnant Church are commanded to be God's bridge between now and the advent! We are the faithful when all else fails! We will prepare to meet our God, and when he triumphantly returns, we will stand as the ones who are ready for him, though all the world is at war, though all have abandoned Him, we will remain! We must remain sanctified! Uninfected by the evils that cause chaos throughout our land! We alone can stop it. We alone through thought and deed can prevent it! For as the book of Revelation tells us, 'but as for the cowardly, the faithless, the detestable, as for murderers, the sexually immoral, sorcerers, idolaters, and all the liars, their portion will be in the lake that burns with fire and sulfur, which is the second death!' We must be pure! We must abstain from being anything that God hates! So 'if your hand causes you to sin, cut it off! It is better to enter life crippled than with two hands, go to Hell, to the unquenchable fire! And if your foot causes you to sin, cut it off too! It is better for you to enter life lame than with two feet, and be thrown into Hell!' As John tells us 'For an hour is coming when all who are in the tombs will hear His voice!' We must be ready! We must see to it that the second Advent is successful!"

Breathing heavily, red faced, and sweating, he stepped down from the pulpit and stood off to the side. The piano started playing and we filed out. Just as every Saturday. I looked at the clock as it ticked by in the narthex. I had half an hour until the lady's group, and I wanted nothing more than to avoid it. Oliver stepped behind me and slipped his arm to interlink with mine. "Hello, beautiful." he said with a smirk on his face. I sighed and shook my head.

"It's as if you are unable to walk up to someone with a proper warning."

"You are as straight laced as your mother would like you to be."

"Not nearly enough, I was slouching." I joked.

"Look at you now, all dolled up, pearls and all. What's the occasion?" he asked.

"My mother is… well, she is finally announcing our engagement at the lady's meeting today." I breathed. My voice turned into a grumble. I looked back to Mama. She stood near a wall, talking to Miss Margaret, the three-time widow.

"She doesn't smile much, does she?" he asked.

I shook my head. "On very few occasions."

"She isn't happy that you're finally getting married?"

"What do you mean by finally? I'm not exactly an old spinster." I huffed, almost pulling my arm away from his.

"So uptight… are you always going to be this way?" he asked lightly.

"Are you always going to be so nagging?" I pushed back.

"Virginia, you need to learn to have fun," he said. He stepped in front and met me with a sly smile. His eyes twinkled with mischievousness.

"You are the most deceptive young man I know." I responded.

He linked arms again and we walked outside. It was one of the most pleasant spring days I had experienced in a while. The sun was so bright that it was almost blinding, but I could still see Oliver's oddly white smile. "And what do you mean by that, may I ask?"

"You're Reverend Perry's nephew. I don't think he likes the idea of fun."

"Not liking the idea of fun?"

"I'm not even sure what fun is." I responded quickly. "But he of all people. When you are around him you stand straight like a well-trained soldier, but when he is not around, you… you act like this!"

"This is nothing," he said. "After we get married, you are going to see what real fun is!" He kissed my cheek.

"That sounds terrifying…" I muttered.

He shook his head and removed his hat. "Oh, Miss Virginia Patterson, you need to lighten up. You are too pretty to get those wrinkles like your mother!"

"Is that all you have to say?" I asked, crossing my arms.

"You told me long ago you wanted me to tell the truth and nothing but the truth!" He put his finger in the air.

"I suppose I did, didn't I? Maybe you telling me all things that are on your mind isn't the best idea."

"I said I would tell the truth," he said, walking towards the blooming apple tree. He picked a blossom and placed it in my hair gently. "I have yet to tell you nearly anything that is going on in my mind. I will though, I will."

"Should I be concerned?" I asked with a smile. He didn't smile back. "I'm assuming that's a yes."

"Virginia!" It was Father's voice bellowing over. I turned around quickly.

Oliver took my hand and kissed it. "I will see you soon, Miss Patterson." He smiled brightly and nodded to me. I hustled over to meet Father. I always preferred his countenance to that of Mama's, but the lady's meeting was with the ladies and Dad's burly figure was anything but lady-like.

"Are we meeting back at home?" I asked Father.

"Yes, and both your siblings will be there to join us in celebrating your engagement." Father said.

"Are they staying all week? The wedding isn't far away." I breathed, saying those words out loud made me nervous.

"Yes, dear," he responded, patting my shoulder before hurrying off.

Mama eyed me again. She was a woman who believed that women should be not seen and not heard, and that's why she wore dark clothing and spoke with her fists and eyes. I went over, trying to walk like she wanted me to. There were lessons we had where she'd take a ruler and smack different parts of my body until I was in the desired shape. She thought that it was very important to be proper, to be an example of perfection at all times. Supposedly it was part of the sanctity we were to achieve. How Father ever managed to survive with someone so cold, I didn't know, but he did, and there was still a smile on his face.

The ladies were all sitting on wooden chairs in the Blue Room, as we called it, merely for a quilt that was made by the ladies in the group which was now hanging on the wall, and the quilt happened to be made of blue material. The room wasn't painted, but it looked pleasant enough with the windows open and the spring sunshine pouring in. The women in the room were of all ages, and not of many varieties. A lot of them were either as hot tempered as Reverend Perry, or as cold and staunch as my mother. Miss Maggie, though, her smile was kind enough that it broke a great tension in the room. She was an amazing 94 years old. She knew a thing or two about life. Even as she was sitting here now with her embroidery in her gnarled and veiny hands, she looked completely in control. She even lived through the Great Disappointment. She had more faith than any of us.

"Good morning, Miss Virginia." Miss Maggie said. I nodded to her and sat down beside Mama. I held onto my shawl just a bit and Mama patted my hands away. They were supposed to be folded in my lap. Mama's face broke into something resembling a smile. "We have good news to tell you all. Virginia is betrothed to Oliver Crain."

"Oh, isn't that wonderful!" Miss Maggie exclaimed.

"Congratulations" And other such compliments were thrown my way.

"It is very important that you are given advice before you go into this. It is dangerous to have no knowledge about what's ahead of you." Elizabeth Miller said. "Now Oliver is a very nice young man. I don't have many worries about him, but men are still men, and men can be very dangerous."

Miss Maggie nodded her head hard as she spoke. "They are tricky creatures. Just remember, you are the strong one. You are the one really in control."

I was getting concerned with the topic, but as Mama said, I wasn't supposed to respond. Just listen. And I was listening. Elizabeth added in, "That is right. As I was saying, men tend to become very animalistic when they are given the opportunity to participate in the marital priviledge. It is part of their nature, but it's unholy. It must be restrained. There must be a balance and that is your role."

Elizabeth's sister Fannie said, "To get that balance you really need to talk to him about what will work. Now, this is a bit of a sensitive topic, and your mother had told me how sensitive you are to things, but the marriage privilege is not to be used lightly, or often. In fact, it can be unhealthy and cause all sorts of problems if you are not looking to be getting a child, and that's all it should be used for. Otherwise the both of you could start acting really strange."

Miss Maggie said, "And you don't need to be putting any undue stress on either of you. If you don't want to have children right away, or anymore after you've had a few, you need to make sure that you don't. After having nine children, I know it can be a problem. It's not fair to you or your children to put them in a situation that isn't good for any of you. Poverty, and a lack of attention are bad on children's little brains."

I was nodding, but starting to realize that I had not even looked at Oliver as someone who I would 'share the marital privilege' with. Considering I only knew that meant 'knowing' one another, I was confused, and a little scared. The women weren't going to talk about the mechanics of the process, they just went on to discuss pregnancy and how strange it made them feel, and then they started to talk about the different foods they wanted to eat, and how long their labor was. Mama didn't say anything at all during the entire time but her face was pleasant enough. It was getting difficult to breathe.

That afternoon when Mama and I returned home, truly I just wanted to take a rest. Although when I saw Miriam and her husband John, and Clarence and his wife Minnie, I was overjoyed. They both still resided in Maine, but without access to leave and visit them, there had been very few chances to see either of them in the past few months and years. Miriam was my younger sister, but she was married when she was 17. She met John in the city while she was working at a hospital. He was a doctor, and almost immediately, they were married. Clarence and Minnie were moving back to Glenborough as she was going to take up a position at the church as a secretary and Clarence was going to help father with the growing business of our general store. "My beautiful little sister, look at you." Clarence clasped his hands on my face.

"I'm very happy you are returning." I said with a smile. "It'll be nice having you around, even if the shenanigans are a little exhaustive."

"I promise you, he hasn't grown out of that yet." Minnie said with a sigh. "And I'm not sure he will."

"Takes after his old man." Father patted him real hard on the back before taking another hug. "Turning into a real man it seems. How was university?"

"Long and informative." he said. "I have learned some very valuable business skills however."

"It was a waste of money…" Mama muttered. "Your job on earth is not to pack up riches."

"Mama, I didn't think that you'd change your mind at any point." Clarence sighed. The atmosphere went from wonderful to uncomfortably electric in a matter of moments. I went towards the cupboard and pulled out the tea cakes I made yesterday, wondering why no one thought to tell me Clarence and Miriam were visiting.

The fighting and complaining never ended well. Father sat down next to Minnie who was listening rather intently to the conversation. "Mother, I made the decision to go because I believed it was important, and I don't regret being there. If anything, it gave me a chance to broaden my horizons. I started a group at school within the Christian Men's Federation to discuss our beliefs. I assisted with their missions. There is a homeless shelter sponsored by the university and the hospital, and I worked quite hard there. That's where I met Minnie."

"It's true Mrs. Patterson." Minnie said. "Your son is a very dedicated man. He was not waning on his faith while doing his studies."

"I didn't ask for your opinion." Mama said harshly. The atmosphere went from electric to just plain awful. It always happened when the family was together. John stood up uncomfortably and went outside. At least Mama liked him, but that was because he never spoke up. She liked silent people, they never argued with her.

"Don't speak to my wife like that." Clarence said with shock pasted all over his face. "Mother, although we both disagree about this subject, can we please manage to be amicable today. We're here to celebrate Virginia's betrothal, not for you to complain about me." Mama looked behind her for a moment. She didn't like to accept defeat. She waved him off and went to her room. She would probably be sulking there all day. Miriam went outside to retrieve John. "I apologize about that Virginia." Clarence said with a heavy sigh.

"I apologize that she acted like that…" I said plainly.

Father said, "Don't either of you take it personally, she's always like this, even more so now that you're all growing up."

"I'm not sure there's any 'more so' about it." Clarence responded with a heavy sigh.

Chapter Two

"Will you stay still Virginia?" Minnie asked. I stared out the window, watching a bluebird hop on a branch while it was happily chirping. It didn't seem to care about anything, just enjoying the bright sun, and the warm wind. I wanted so badly to be outside. "I have a lot of work to do, my sister wasn't exactly a small person." The dress she was hemming for me was her sister's wedding dress. Her sister had died of influenza a few months ago, and Minnie was more than happy to allow me to wear it. "And you, Virginia, are. Did you not eat your vegetables growing up?"

"Uh…" I muttered, losing track of the bluebird.

Clarence just laughed and said from the kitchen, "I think something stunted her."

"Thank you," I said sarcastically. I took in a deep breath and tried to focus on staying in place. She poked at the dress with pins, and I wasn't a fan of needles.

"You are going to be gorgeous, Virginia." Miriam said when she walked in.

Clarence said, "Isn't she already?"

"Thank you, Clarence." I said with a smile, almost blushing. Although at the moment I looked more like a porcupine in this dress.

"Oliver is a lucky young man."

"You used to say that you'd take a gun to anyone who liked me."

"Stop moving," Minnie said.

"Yes, but Oliver is harmless." Clarence responded.

"Harmless is a loaded word." I replied. "I do love him though."

"Marriage is a strange thing." Minnie said.

"Strange?" Clarence interjected.

"It's like picking one person to jump into the future with, having to see them day in and day out, trusting them with everything." she said quietly, taking scissors to the bottom hem.

"I suppose it is strange." Clarence replied quietly. "It's nice though. I think it is." He stepped up closer. "And you won't be far away, will you?"

"No, no, no, Oliver lives on some land right next to ours. It belongs to Reverend Perry, but he's been working to buy it from him."

"And he does what?" Miriam asked.

"He's a banker." I said. "But he has a small farm. Nothing special, he raises chickens and sells the meat and eggs to Father. I will still be working with Father at the store."

"Looks like we'll be seeing a lot of each other." Clarence said with a smile.

Miriam threaded together some spring flowers to make a headband, practicing for the wedding day. I watched the wind blow through the pine trees outside, listening to the constant twittering of birds. I could see Oliver walking through his land. Just seeing him, I smiled. There was a dog, out of sight, that was ceaselessly barking. "Will that thing ever be quiet?" Miriam asked, lying her head on the table.

"You are far less patient than I." I said with a smile.

"Yes, yes, I am. I'm not sure I could ever stand the sound of a baby crying." she said with a shudder. "And they look so breakable."

"You don't want children then?" I asked. She shook her head.

"No, no, thankfully John doesn't either. If we do, we're adopting. Considering how the world is decaying as it is, I feel that the birth of a child would be more... of an event of grief than love." She responded shrugging. "That's only our opinion. I don't want to sway you."

"I don't have an opinion," I said.

"You truly are what Mother wishes you to be." Clarence said with a sigh. "You need to get away, and when you do, get some opinions for yourself. You're perfectly able to make decisions." He moved so he was sitting beside me and made eye contact. He smiled a bit, easing the remaining tension in the house. I nodded. "You don't need to be silent."

After the day's visit, it was only a week until the actual wedding celebration. I never thought I would be so nervous for something so simple, but thankfully Miss Maggie made the church look and smell delicious, and Father even brought a camera to take a wedding photograph of Oliver and I. Minnie made her sister's wedding dress fit me, and oddly enough, I felt quite beautiful in it. Miriam's final crown of flowers was on my head, attached to a long veil and the veil was as long as the dress, which floated just above the floor, with careful hemming of course. The entire congregation was invited, and with the promise of free food and some entertainment, I was sure they'd come. I could see Oliver's family as well, many people with the countenance of Amos Perry were walking about like thin giants, giants who were in desperate need for some food.

The weather, though, unfortunately, wasn't the best today. God decided it should be cloudy, although not raining.

The sun was desperately trying to peak through the clouds, but to no avail. The birds still sang though, and I could see a flock huddled in the trees as if they were going to watch the ceremony too. Miss Maggie and Miriam put flowers all over the outside of the church, and on the inside as well to make it look very much like spring. I was thankful, it made up for the dreary conditions outdoors. I realized though, that I hardly thought about this day actually occurring, or what it would be like. It only seemed like a distant must, in the future of course, but currently, it was the present. Every second that ticked by was cutting further into the day, and I didn't know what to think. For no reason, my nerves started to dig through my flesh and make me uncomfortable. It wasn't Oliver, nor the church, nor the people here, the nerves were just doing as they pleased.

The church pianist, Ruth, was playing a pretty melody. Everyone sat down in the sanctuary on the wooden benches. All except for Oliver who was standing near Amos Perry, and my father and I in the narthex. I held flowers in my hands, they matched the ones in the crown. My Father had his arm wrapped around mine. "How are you feeling, Ginny?" he asked.

"I don't know…" I muttered.

"I'm here, right beside you." he said. His voice was always comforting, it sounded like there were trumpets behind it. Today he stood very tall, and proud, his chest puffed out a little more than normal. He was wearing his best suit with a hat Mama bought him for their anniversary. He hardly ever wore it for fear that it'd get ruined. "I'm very proud of you Ginny," he said.

"For what? I haven't done anything yet." I said with a smile looking back at him.

"For becoming such a wonderful young lady."

"I'm not going that far away. I'm still going to help you at the store."

"Yes, but you won't be under my roof any longer, you won't be my little girl."

"I'll always be your little girl," I responded, hugging him tightly.

He seemed far more prepared to walk down the aisle than I. The light poured through the glass windows. The clouds dissipated some. Oliver looked at me with the brightest smile upon his face. There were little dimples on his cheeks. His chest puffed out too, just like Father's. Oliver looked rather comical in his suit though. I'd never seen him so dressed up, but come to think of it, he's never seen me wear a wedding dress with a crown of flowers on my head and a veil, so we probably both looked a little foolish.

Father handed me off to Oliver. Father's head went down a bit, but a smile remained, and he sat down next to Mama, who was slouching just a very small bit. We took hands and Amos Perry stood between us, still a tower of judgement. I could feel him breathe. I could hear him swallow as he spoke. "Today we are all witnesses, gathered together to celebrate the sacrament of marriage between Oliver Crain and Virginia Patterson. As we stand as the remnant church, patiently awaiting the judgement of God, we continue on with the plan he has ordained for us: the beauty of family. In the Book of Genesis, it states, 'Therefore a man shall leave his father and his mother, and hold fast to his wife, and they shall become one flesh.' 'Husbands, love your wives, as Christ loved the church, and gave himself up for her, that he might sanctify her, having cleansed her by the washing of water with the word, so that he might present the church to himself in splendor, without spot or wrinkle or any such thing, that she might be holy and without blemish. In the same way husbands should love their wives as their own bodies. He who loves his wife loves himself.'" Oliver squeezed my hands a little bit, and never broke eye contact.

"We love because He first loved us." Reverend Perry said with a booming voice. "In the book of Corinthians it states: 'If I speak in the tongues of men and of angels, but have not love, I am a noisy gong or a clanging cymbal. And if I have prophetic powers, and understand all mysteries and all knowledge, and if I have all faith, so as to move mountains, but have not love, I am nothing! Love is patient, and kind; love does not envy or boast; it is not arrogant, or rude. It does not insist on its own way; it is not irritable, or resentful. It does not rejoice at wrong doing, but rejoices with the truth. Love bears all things, believes all things, hopes all things, endures all things." Amos Perry took a deep breath and said, "Now shall we present the rings," The amount of debate it took to decide if we would have rings or not weighed heavy on me. Half the people in this room thought that the wearing of rings was ostentatious and unnecessary. Oliver took them from the pocket of his suit. I was looking at real gold. "These rings symbolize faithfulness through all afflictions, difficulties, and joy, and represent your bond through all of life, until death do you part."

Oliver placed the ring on my finger, and I placed his ring on his finger. "You may now kiss the bride." Amos said quietly. For a very brief moment, we kissed. I'd never kissed Oliver before. Panicked, I realized that I was no longer myself.

The remaining day was a blur of activity. I stayed near Oliver's side as much as possible, but there were so many people wishing to speak to us. Miss Maggie stayed near me and if I looked flustered she shooed them away. She was the rock through all of this hurried madness. Her happy wrinkled face and quick reflexes kept me at ease, that and I could freely hold onto Oliver's arm tightly and no one would question if we were being holy or not, it was holy matrimony after all.

The sun did remain in the sky, although occasionally blocked by thick stubborn clouds. I only wished to look at the pretty formations of the clouds and the bright blue that colored the sky, and the flowers that were lining the church, and sit here at a rustic table and eat past my fill. The food was wonderful since it came from Maggie's hands, but I had no appetite. I only wished to get away from the church and home. Then I realized home wasn't home anymore and that Father and Clarence were both gone for some time during the meal. They were moving my things over to Oliver's house. My stomach then started to churn with those nerves coming and going. I wouldn't even be able to relax in a familiar environment. Of course, I had been to Oliver's home once or twice, accompanied by a family member, but it was not a lasting visit.

Oliver was happy and smiling and talking to the congregation members. "Are you alright, Virginia?" he asked, eyeing me.

"Oh yes," I replied, questioning if I was lying or not. I didn't even know.

He kissed my cheek. "This will all be done soon."

"And I will be thankful for that." It was getting to be mid-afternoon when people started to dissipate. Miss Maggie still had more energy than I could ever have. I was drained, but she made sure that all her food was eaten. I was so full that I could hardly move. "Thank you for all your help, Miss Maggie." I said to her. I took her hand in mine, the familiar cold, smoothness of an elderly person's hand touching mine. "I could not have seen this day happen so well without you."

"Oh you are so very welcome, Mrs. Crain!" she said, kissing my cheek before whisking up her dishes" to the church kitchen.

"Mrs. Crain…" I muttered.

"Sounds strange?" Oliver asked with a smile.

"Far too strange." I smiled a bit.

Oliver and I walked into the house, hearing the door creak closed behind me. My feet were firmly on the wooden ground. My belongings were piled neatly in the living room, a chest of clothing, some dresses, quilts, but little else. It was odd to see how little I personally owned. I sat down on the couch and sunk in. "I am so tired!" I exclaimed.

"Look at you, so lazy!" Oliver said, laughing. "Your mother would never stand for this!"

"My mother isn't here to stop me…" I muttered.

"What is this Virginia I'm seeing?" he chuckled, sliding to sit next to me. "Such a rare sight indeed!" I placed my head on his shoulder for a brief moment before removing the flower crown. "There are petals in your hair." Oliver said. I shook my head and they floated down to my dress and onto the wooden floor. "I have something to show you." He stood up quickly, once again filled with energy.

I stood up slower and took a hold of his arm. We went the large open kitchen and he opened the cupboards lining the walls. Beautiful china plates and crystal cups filled the shelves. "Where did you get all of this, Oliver?" I asked. "It's gorgeous."

"I have been saving for ten years." he said. "I wanted to make this house perfect for you and our families."

"Oh Oliver…" I muttered, opening other cupboards, there were glass vases, and sturdy stoneware, and silver forks and spoons carefully packed in a wooden box. Even the kitchen table was beautiful with a lacey covering. It was slightly yel-lowed, but had clearly lived through quite a few generations. I sat at one of the chairs, and touched the table. It was mine. I would be able to look at this for the rest of forever, to build our lives together. When I stood, we walked through the house, looking at all the wonders he collected throughout the years, including a heavy, cherry desk at the edge of the living room with a porcelain lamp sitting on it. "I really don't know what to say..." I breathed, holding up a perfect quilt hanging from a quilt holder on the wall.

Oliver wrapped his arms around me from the back and kissed my cheek. "You don't need to say anything,"

I turned around with a smile on my face. "I'm a little cu-rious." I breathed. I touched my lips to his for a moment, and his arms became tighter around my body. "Although whatever plans you seem to have in that mind of yours, please postpone them." I made eye contact with him. "I just want to sleep." He sighed heavily.

I went into the washroom to dress for bed although it was a little early. A porcelain washbasin sat underneath a mirror with a dressing stool behind it. I'd never been in such a beautiful space before, and I felt surprisingly comfortable. I unbraided my hair, letting it fall loose and wispy over my shoulders. In the mirror my eyes looked glassy and dark. I wondered why I was so dull and slow in comparison to Oliver's brightness. I exited the washroom, which was just adjacent to the bedroom, and Oliver was already in bed. He was reading a newspaper by the light of a lamp. "We aren't supposed to read that," I said, startling him.

"There's a lot of things you don't know, Virginia, but the least of which is that I enjoy reading the newspaper." Oliver sighed.

I sat beside him stiffly. "Then why don't you tell me all those secrets then, since we're married?" I breathed, trying to relax. That word: married, still sounded odd to me. It almost sounded fake.

"One is good enough for today." he said, folding it back up. There was a comb beside me, it was bright blue and sparkling with the golden light of that lamp.

"This is beautiful as well. Oliver, you thought of everything..." I sighed and looked at it closer. "I feel as if I have put no effort into this marriage while you..."

"There's nothing to worry about." Oliver pressed. "Please, just enjoy all of this. That's the purpose, I gathered these things together for you to enjoy. This way it's your house too."

"This is all too strange... I'm not used to there... being any one beside me in bed, much less a man." I lay my head back against the headboard.

"Seems you'll have to get used to it yes?" he said with a smirk.

"Just haven't been in close proximity to... well, men before."

"Even your father and brother?" he asked. "There's not a lot of difference between us, just..." He seemed to wiggle around a bit. "This." He lifted up the quilt and revealed the he had slipped out of his trousers. I held my hand up to my face.

"Oh God, Oliver, what are you doing?"

"Well that's the only difference." he said with a huff.

"Put the quilt down and get your trousers back on please! And where are your nickers?" I asked, voice rising. I couldn't help but laugh though.

"It's not that scary."

"Looks like a skinned rabbit..." I whispered.

"What?" he asked, edging his face a little closer.

"Nothing, nothing, I didn't say anything. Please, God, please, get your trousers back on. I don't want to see that again."

"It's not that bad, Ginny!" he cried. "Fine, fine, fine… but you're going to have to get used to it! We're married!"

"They warned me about this…" I said, shaking my head, still, for some odd reason, a smile pasted across my face.

"Who?"

"The lady's group, said men were animals."

"Aw, I'm not an animal," he said, kissing my cheek. I think he was getting back into his trousers. "I promise."

"You promise what?"

"Not to be an animal."

"I'm not even sure what that entails." I said.

"Neither do I."

Chapter Three

Oliver and I were awarded but one day to ourselves before returning to 'normal' life. Tomorrow Oliver would return to work at the bank, and I would go to my Father's general store. In the meantime, though, we were cleaning the house. While I was in the bedroom, I stretched the quilt tightly over the bed, smoothing it out, tucking in the edges. The crisp white, embroidered pillows were fluffed, laying one next to the other against the simple headboard. As I did that, my toe touched something beneath the bed. There was an old trunk underneath Oliver's half of the bed. "What is this, Oliver?" I asked.

He ran in and said, "Don't touch it! Please!" He held his hands in the air before shoving it right back where it was. His face suddenly turned sweaty and red before he crossed his arms and stepped back.

"Why are you acting so strange?" I asked.

He took in a deep breath. "I'll let you know what's in there, when... when I believe I can trust you with the information."

"And when would that be?"

"When you can trust me." he responded quietly, touching my hand.

"In what way..." I muttered, crossing my arms.

"Please, Ginny, just leave the trunk be."

"Fine, I will. I will. I don't want to make you so uncomfortable, but you need to be able to tell me everything. That's the only way I can think a marriage can work well."

"I know, but I can be fearful sometimes, just like anyone else." he responded.

"You don't need to be afraid around me." I said, hugging him tightly.

"Isn't that all people do, go around judging?"

"That's not what we're supposed to do." I responded quietly and sat down on the bed. I liked touching the embroidery on the quilt, it was calming. "People are supposed to be welcoming. That's why we were put on this earth, not to be destructive. Judging is destructive."

"It is." he said. "God, I love you." He smiled brightly and picked me up off the bed and kissed me. I'd never been this close to a person before, any person, since I was a toddler probably. My arms were comfortably around his neck and I warmly kissed him back. It was an odd experience, I truly didn't see the purpose to kissing, the exchange of saliva was disgusting actually, but part of me did enjoy it. There was an electricity going throughout my body and I was very aware of everything, and anything. Not only Oliver but myself, and everything around us. The most concerning part was the fact that Oliver also seemed to know what he was doing, if this was in fact the marital privilege, which is what I assumed it was. But it also was a comfort because I was so confused. I just wanted to know what was in that trunk. Curiosity in many respects was a very powerful thing, and so was the lack of thought. Thought was becoming kind of an inhibitor, and as Oliver said, I needed to stop allowing myself to be inhibited.

"I'm not sure what that was…" I muttered, turning to him as I lay on my back, staring at the ceiling, both of us breathing heavily and raggedy. He chuckled and faced me, placing his hand on my cheek. "Oh, no, get that away, I know where that's been." I flicked his hand away and cringed. "God…"

"You are your mother's prude!" he said with a laugh. "I should have expected that."

"Expected what?" I sat up and crossed my arms, careful to keep myself as covered as possible, although I wasn't sure why I found myself so concerned with my image. "I didn't know what to expect." I put my head on his chest, listening to his heart slow, beating evenly along, swiftly, smoothly. He placed his hand on my head and combed through my hair.

"Just think, we have our entire lives ahead of us…"

"You think so big."

"Learned from the best…" he said, looking up to the ceiling as if it was the sky. "But really, think about it."

"And you were dreaming about this ten years ago?"

"I knew I wanted to marry you. No other girl would go run through the fields with me and hop through the crick." He chuckled. "Even with the looming doom of your mother hanging over you, you still did it and would come back with all the courage you could muster when you were all muddy; ready and waiting for that stick."

"You make it sound positive." I said.

"I didn't know anyone else who was like that."

"And you say that I don't know how to have fun…" I muttered.

"Then your mother wouldn't let you leave, stuck you in that house with embroidery lessons. You looked so miserable."

"That's because I was miserable." I said. "She's awful… I still don't know how Miriam put up with her like that."

"Your sister is as quiet as a little mouse." Oliver added. "She's knows how not to be seen or heard…"

"Just what Mother ordered. I don't know why she would want anyone to be like that." I sat up a bit more, straining to stretch my arms. "It doesn't make sense. Wouldn't any mother want to raise strong children able to… to take on the world or something like that?"

"She's loves tradition, however stupid and shitty that tradition is."

My eyes went wide. "Going with some bad words there, Oliver."

"Oh yes, I'm going to burn in hell, I already know that." Oliver said with a heavy breath and a smile on his face.

"Oh, don't say that," I said, smacking his arm a bit. "I really need to get up and work on the garden."

"You won't stay a bit longer?" he asked.

"There's things to do Oliver…" I grumbled, swinging my legs over and onto the woven rug the bed stood on. Oliver lay down with a heavy sigh, waving his arms idly in the air. I knelt down and pulled my dressing gown on quickly before entering the washroom. I closed the door behind me. White light entered the small window above, enough that I didn't need to light the lamp. I sat down on the dressing stool, and pulled the blue comb through my frazzled, messy hair. My face was flushed. I touched my cheek and splashed it with water before braiding my hair tightly. The dress was heavy, almost too much for outdoor work, but nonetheless, tied my boots on tightly with the skirt of my dress floating just above the ankles. When I left the washroom, Oliver was still lying in bed, content as could be.

Outside was my new beautiful garden. It was twice the size of the one at my parent's house and stretched across the green space between the house and the edge of the wood. Chickens pecked outside the garden, straying from the chicken coop. The weather was reasonable today, just a bit windy and partially sunny. Little rays cut through thick clumps of clouds. As I approached the garden, lugging a few wooden buckets of gardening supplies. Up against the chicken wire fence of the garden I went through the burlap sacks of seeds. It was time to start sowing the garden. I wondered if Oliver was still lazily lying in bed, however, humming a hymn I went on, planting the garden. Tomatoes, beans, pumpkins, peas, radishes, anything we had seeds for and would be edible. There were marigolds to plant around the edges to help keep animals away from the garden, except for the fact that chickens enjoyed eating marigold blossoms. Back home, the marigolds sometimes grew so large that they'd go up to my knees, and bear some of the largest flowers I'd ever seen, all beautiful fall colors.

After hours of kneeling and digging in the dirt, I fed the chickens, flinging them their seed before filling their water dish. I still hadn't seen Oliver, but the day was waning and the sunset was becoming rather strong and radiant, spreading across the sky in various oranges and pinks. When I went inside, I realized how dirty I was, and to avoid carrying the soil into the house, I knocked off my boots before entering and washing my hands. Expecting that I'd have to get dinner ready, I was surprised to see Oliver in the kitchen, standing over the stove, stirring something. "What are you doing?" I asked lightly.

He turned around and said, "I thought you'd be hungry after all that work."

I sat at the kitchen table, smiling. "You're so special."

"Hah," he said with a laugh. "I'm glad you think that."

Chapter Four

I had a normal marriage within our first few days. Although I didn't know what normal was supposed to be. I did have trust, for the most part, with Oliver, which was all I truly wished for. We both understood that we could be honest with one another, a situation we had never found ourselves in before.

A routine, though, was quickly concocted. The morning was filled with slow moving and washing up. I'd get my hair braided while Oliver very carefully shaved. "You don't want a beard?" I asked him as he placed the razor blade against his taut cheek. When we released the pressure he said, "Unless I want to look like a mangy dog, I'd like to keep my face smooth."

"A mangy dog?" I asked.

"I'm not going to get a nice full beard like your father, or Clarence. It's just not happening." He turned his head slightly, starting on the other cheek.

"At least it's not a skinned rabbit."

"Are you trying to make me cut myself?" he asked with a laugh. "This is a knife."

"I see it's a knife." I responded, spinning my hair into a bun, pinning it tightly to my head.

After that we both went outside to care for the chickens. The air was chilled and humid. Everything was covered with dew. Oliver and I each had a large bucket of chicken feed and scattered it for the children before gathering the eggs. With what time was left we had eat breakfast. Today and nearly every day afterwards, it was usually toast and eggs, sometimes bacon, and if we were lucky, a strudel cake. Then we both left in the cart and headed to the general store where I started my day with my Father and Clarence, while Oliver went to the bank.

The second day at work, Clarence met with me inside the general store. He hugged me and said, "How are you doing?"

"Well," I said, passing by the store space into the kitchen in the back. "And are you happy being home now?"

"I'm glad Minnie and I have some space from Mother though, she's still being hostile."

"It's been a week since that argument." I sighed.

"You know she likes to hold grudges."

"And yet she spits scripture at us." I said, crossing my arms after placing the basket of eggs on the butcher's block counter.

"I'm sure she means well." he growled.

"Are you just saying that to be a good son?" I asked.

He chuckled and nodded. "Probably. We've got a few orders today coming in." He handed me some yellowing, old paper. Father was a frugal business owner and bought the onion paper in bulk.

"I'll get started on that." I said with a sigh and yawn. Making bread was merely a reflex now with little brain power needed. The scoops of flour, sugar, salt, leavening, mixed with the eggs and water. The mixing and kneading was rhythmic and soothing. It was only a little while of the first pile of dough before my mind started wandering off. It pinpointed the sound of a group of birds outside, singing to one another. I felt trapped inside the store, but work was necessary for food and sustenance. Working was part of being human. Startled, thoughts of Oliver entered my mind, the tracing of his fingers across my skin. I shuddered and shivered in response to the imaginary touch and the simple thoughts.

With the dough set against the warm window to rise, I started on another loaf of bread. A bird flitted to the window, and sat there, singing, looking to me. A little red-breasted robin with a massive belly. It looked like she was going to lay some eggs soon. I gathered up some crumbs and placed them on the window sill. The bird flew away at my sudden movement, but as soon as it felt safe, it approached again. She pecked at the crumbs, and another robin joined her. Distracted, I watched them while my flour dusted hand rested on the loaf of bread dough. "Ginny! Is there bread in the oven?" he called, probably noticing me staring idly at the window. One of the birds flew away at Clarence's voice as it carried into the kitchen. I sighed and returned to work, putting the first loaf into the oven while the second loaf rose. There wasn't a lot of other aspects of my job except for being a functional bakery, me being the only one producing anything. I was always covered in flour. It wasn't a bad existence, it was just what it was.

That night, while Oliver and I were eating dinner I asked, "When can I see what's in that trunk?" I asked.

He sighed and said, "It's only been a few days."

"What's the problem, Oliver? What are you scared of?"

"I don't know."

"Is this just a game or something?" I asked, leaning back in my chair, my arms crossed briefly.

He shook his head. "No," he said, sipping at the stew. I dunked a thick piece of bread into the chicken broth a few times.

"Then what is happening here?" I asked.

"I don't want to make things uncomfortable." He said. "I just want to have a normal marriage."

"When did you expect this to be normal?" I asked.

"We should do something." he immediately said. "Something fun,"

"Of course…" I muttered. "There's no time for that yet, Oliver."

"On Sunday, we should do something on Sunday."

I sighed but agreed. "Surprise me."

Simply, though, I didn't like surprises. They made me uncomfortable and nervous. With so much time to think, all the speculations swimming around in my head during work just made the smallest thing a bit maddening. There were so many mysteries, that of what Oliver was hiding in the trunk, what he planned for Sunday, and the ever-present questioning of what exactly the marriage privilege was. It was called sex, but that was all I knew, and that its purpose was to have children. Oliver and I hadn't talked about children yet. My assumption was we'd have them. The house was so large, and quiet, it felt like it needed to be filled with some laughter and warmth. I could be a better mother than my own. I wouldn't use a stick to force my child into the correct positions, making them silent, and invisible. I always thought that was cruel.

Over the week, Father was less and less at the counter, that was becoming Clarence's job, and I kept good record of what was sold and what was ordered from outside the little town. Father was thinking of implementing a pharmacy section of our shop that he thought I would be able to run, we'd have to hire someone else to make the baked goods. Clarence was suggesting that Minnie's younger sister could take the position, but the girl was only sixteen. Until Father completed his business decisions, I was kept busy in the back making orders of baked goods for my neighbors. Mrs. Annette Garrison came in every other day for a large loaf of wheat bread. She liked the

crust extra thick, just like I did. Miss Maggie came in about
once a week for a pie, the pie depended on her mood, but it
was shared at a quilting club hosted at her house just down
the street from the church. Although most people made their
bread and other goods themselves, I still sold a good 50 loaves
a week, as well as cookies, and rolls. I was kept very busy.

The little room I was in still allowed me to hear the little
bell ring whenever anyone came in. Clarence was learning
everyone's names. His memory was poor, and after the five
years of being away from home, even in the town that never
changed, he started losing track of people. In the store, though,
there would always be talking and laughter. I hoped I could
save up enough money to bring a radio in the store so I could
listen to some music while working. I was thankful for the
window in the room. I needed the fresh air. There was nothing
I hated more than being away from nature. I already felt as if
I was separate enough. If I could, I'd spend every day lying
in thick, soft tufts of grass, watching the clouds go by and
listening to birds.

I was placing bread in the baskets outside when Amos
Perry walked in. The air changed with his presence. Instead of
the joviality that pervaded the air before, it became rough and
stale. He looked as stern as ever. I made the communion bread,
just as every week, but I never enjoyed his visits. He nodded to
me and removed his hat. He always did that around ladies. I
retrieved his bread and he put the money on the counter near
Clarence. "I pray that everything is well between you and my
nephew?"

"Yes sir." I responded. "We are doing well."

"And I hope to see you on Saturday, yes? Together?"

"Of course, sir." I said. Oliver was not the best at attending
church regularly, never since he was thirteen and his father

died. His mother was broken by that and there was no one to pressure him into going. He preferred staying home, working on the land. He didn't like being around his uncle. I'm not sure anyone actually did. At any point in my life, though, I didn't have a choice. Mother was such a stickler to make sure we were there and at our best that I had never missed a Saturday, even though I was born on a Friday. Even at one day old I was in a pew. Oliver, on the other hand, came maybe once a month at best. The only services he didn't miss was Christmas Day, and Easter. He was a very flighty man. His mind was here there and everywhere but the now, and often that meant he didn't really know what day it was.

"I hope to see that you keep that young man in line." Reverend Perry said deeply.

"Yes, sir." I said, nodding to him. I backed up a bit, hoping to return to my work. His stare was uncomfortable, boring right into me before he quickly placed his hat back on his head and returned outside.

Clarence looked over to me. "Odd man, isn't he? Are you alright, Virginia?" he asked.

I nodded. "He scares me some." I admitted, returning to the doorway of the room.

"It's Friday, he is always here on Friday." Clarence said. "I'm glad you had his order finished on time, though."

"I missed once. Once." I cried out, laughing. "And you will hold it against me for how long?"

"As long as I still find his reaction amusing!" Clarence smiled a bit, and sat back down on his seat. A few months ago, I failed to finished the communion bread on time for Reverend Perry due to excess orders considering it being almost Christmas (apparently my grandmother Ethel's Christmas cookie recipe was very popular), and I thought he'd burn the whole place down spewing his fire and brimstone speech. I always thought that one of these days I'd see the true Reverend Perry and his tongue would actually be made of fire.

When it was getting near time for me to leave I cleaned up the room and cooled the oven. I stepped out and stood near Clarence. "So how are you and Minnie doing?" I asked.

"Very well, very well." he said with a smirk. "I can see just by the way you are walking that you have changed some."

"Why are you analyzing the way I am walking?" I asked, suddenly standing still.

"It's not a bad thing, Ginny. It doesn't help that we are in the same building all day together." he added simply. "I think that Oliver is going to help you become… more human, I guess."

"Are you suggesting I'm not sufficiently human now?" I asked.

He shook his head. There was some fuzz on his chin. He was always failing at trying to grow a proper beard out like Father. A brief thought came to mind that he may want to stop trying to do as Oliver did, quit and shave it off to save the eye sore that was the ugly fluff that occasionally dotted the edges of his ever-rounding chin. "That's not what I said. I said more human, not just human. There's a difference."

"I should take the ledger for today." I said, hoping the change of topic would be successful enough to actually change the topic. "I'll get everything for the week tallied up this weekend. Is there anything you know you need ordered? That you are sure of this time?" I wasn't the only one that made mistakes. The amount of lard Clarence ordered one time led to an overage that was nearly impossible to deal with in a reasonable manner, and Father throwing one of the few fits I'd ever seen him throw.

"Sugar." he said. "The people around here seem to have an insatiable need for sugar. My mind isn't really working right now however, so you'll just look at the ledger and decide from there. You have better judgement than I." I didn't believe him when it came to that, but sat down with the ledger at the desk behind the tall wooden counter.

Oliver opened the door, making the little brass doorbell ring. I stood up quickly, looking over the desk, almost on my tip-toes to see. He was carrying flowers. I quickly stepped up to him and kissed his cheek before taking the flowers. "You didn't forget about our plans for this evening, did you?" he asked.

"In fact I may have…" I muttered quietly. "I thought we were going out on Sunday,"

"Well, I've changed my mind. We're going to a real restaurant first." He pulled on my hand gently and kissed my cheek again.

Clarence shook his head with a sly smile and said, "I need that ledger done before you go anywhere, Ginny."

I grumbled and went behind the counter, Oliver following me. He was wearing surprisingly nice clothes for such an occasion, although recently it seemed that he decided that now he was a married man he might as well look the part of a grown professional. He was wearing a nice gray wool suit. If he wasn't so used to it, he'd probably be dying of heat. I was thankful I could wear my light loose cotton dress, although I thought it'd look nice with a hat, I still feared that if Mama saw me in one she'd scold me for being too ostentatious. Oliver even wore a hat, I think he felt more comfortable with the coverage on his hair. He was uncomfortable about his hair and how unruly it was without that jelly stuff in his hair to keep it in place. He called it a Homburg hat, but it wasn't my favorite one, the nice grey cap he had was the best looking one on.

I finished the ledger and wrote out the orders before leaving. Clarence patted me on the back, and Oliver wrapped an arm around my waist and pulled me up against him. If there was anyone else around, I'd be terribly uncomfortable with this public display of affection, and yet I just wanted to kiss him as soon as we sat on the bench in the cart. I put my head in the crook of his neck and he chuckled. The laughter reverberated through his body warmly. "I feel like you're trying to make this a special occasion." I said.

"Everything should be a special occasion. Makes life fun."

"I'm covered in flour." I said with a sigh, trying to dust myself off as we pulled onto the dirt road.

As we pulled into town, we entered the corner of the square. It was late afternoon, the golden light cut through rolling clouds. Oliver urged the horse forward, and the clicking of the hooves against the road was and always had been, quite comforting. One of the only true restaurants of any worth in Glenborough Maine, the Cuckoo's Nest, was in this area. No one in my family dared to come here because the owner of it was part of an Irish Catholic family, and supposedly, according to Mama, she said they were trash. I didn't know where she got that idea from, but I had high hopes for their food. Any food I didn't have to make myself probably tasted extraordinary, as long as Miriam wasn't cooking it.

Oliver parked the cart in front of the Cuckoo's Nest and helped me down. We entered the space, and I was hit by a rich smell. Up on the walls were pictures of advertisements from magazines and newspapers. "My mother would kill you if she knew what was in this place." I whispered. A man greeted us, looking just as dapper as Oliver, with his hair neatly smoothed back. Oliver removed his hat and held it against his stomach, one of his hands still holding onto my arm. The man led us to a booth, and we received cold water. Oliver smiled and said, "Cold water and it's not even winter."

"It's like you've never seen an ice box before." I said. "There's one in the kitchen."

"I bought it a week before the wedding. It's new." he said, sipping the water.

"When will I see what's in that trunk?"

"You won't rest, will you?" he asked with a heavy sigh, shaking his head.

"When will you trust me?" I asked.

"I do trust you."

"I don't believe you since I still don't know what's in there. What could possibly be so bad…?"

"It's bad." he said, crossing his arms defensively.

"Did you bring me here so we can just argue?" I whispered.

"We aren't arguing, we're just talking." he said staunchly.

"Do I still need to wait until Saturday?"

"Yes." he said. Next to us there was a few advertisements on the wall. One was for woman's clothes patterns. Looking closely, all the women had black short hair, no longer than their chins. All the women in photographs on this wall were short like that. Most also had large, floppy hats, or those close to their head with bows. They looked so foreign and different. No one in our community looked like these girls with cosmetics and color all over their faces and greasy hair that wasn't in braids.

I pointed at one of the women on the wall and said, "Look at that hair, it's like a man's."

"I don't know many men with hair like that." he said with a smile.

"It's so short. There's nothing hardly to pull a brush through, nothing to braid."

"It's easier to keep clean and smooth," he said. "You used to complain about your hair all the time."

"I don't know if it'd be better to have more manageable hair or not having to listen to my mother."

"You're a married woman. You shouldn't have to listen to your mother." he said with a heavy sigh.

"That's easier said than done." I responded as the waiter came by and gave us the food. "What is this? I didn't order."

"I know, I took the liberty." He said with a sly smile. "It's a roast."

"There's meat in it." I said.

"I realize that." We weren't supposed to eat meat. "Just try it."

My eyes went wide for a moment and my stomach was happy. The flavor nearly exploded in my mouth.

"She's not ruling over you." he said.

"According to Reverend Perry, she is and should be." I said with a sigh.

"There's a reason I don't go there very often." he whispered. "Maybe we should try going to another church."

"I haven't missed a service in years," I said.

Oliver stood up and said, "I'll be right back."

"Where are you going?" I asked.

"Just one moment," he pressed, and he went up to the main counter of the restaurant and talked to the man who welcomed us into the busy establishment. Oliver's face lit up and he returned to the booth.

"What were you doing?"

"I asked the man what time his church services were, at the Catholic church down the road."

I shook my head, my face flushing with heat. "What are you thinking?" I whispered.

"What? It wouldn't hurt to get you out, see something different. I have a friend who's Catholic."

"What time is it?" I asked.

"It's at eight on Sunday."

"That's a lot of church." I said with a sigh. "If they find out that we went there..." I shook my head.

"I'm sure they won't be yelling at us nearly as much as Perry."

"What are you trying to do to me?" I asked, my voice just above a whisper.

"Nothing bad." he said, leaning back with a smirk on his face. "You just need to try new things, decide for yourself."

"If I was allowed to decide for myself, I would've ordered food for myself."

"Would you have been willing to try meat?" he asked. I sighed. "See? I know what I'm talking about. I know you well."

Chapter Five

All seemed to have returned to life as it was before marriage when I was sitting in that pew beside my mother on Saturday morning. While I sat with my back as straight as humanly possible, Oliver slumped a bit next to me. We finished singing the third hymn and the organ quieted as Reverend Perry went up to his pulpit. His face was papery white, and yet heavy with age. His jowls looked like that of a dog, and he eyed Oliver sharply. If Amos Perry was ever surprised at anything, it was that Oliver had been to church three weekends in a row. Maybe he'd think I was a good role model for my husband. If he knew anything about Oliver, he'd realize that he'd be what he called an apostate. A liar. And yet I didn't feel as if Oliver was bad in any way. He just was the way he was.

"In times like these we must remember who we are as a community and what we stand for. We believe in the Word of God. We are Bible believing Christians, we are not locked in the Dark Times, while truth was getting its head dashed against a stone, listening to the Anti-Christ. We believe that God can speak to people through his messengers! Why not? Why would we believe that God has remained silent? Thus we understand that people like Ms. Ellen White gained many visions from God, giving us our prophesy, inspired like the Bible.

Imagine having been able to speak with angels! Imagine God choosing you to speak to his chosen ones!" I was interrupted by my mother jabbing her fist into my thigh. My heart jumped just slightly and I realized how much I didn't want to be here.

"Just as Ms. White said, it is our sacred duty to attend to our health, to keep our passions in check, to live in a healthful, and clean way, to live a temperate life. Self-control will always be man's greatest glory. We must believe in moderation in all things; we must attend to our bodies as they are the temples of God's spirit. While I believe most of you have good intentions in your life, I don't believe you are working hard enough to keep your body pure. You pollute your bodies with gravies, and fried foods, butter, and pastries, and rich cheese, meat, and milk. Your diet should be of whole grain breads, vegetables, fruits, nuts, and the healing power of water! This is a holy cause my people! This is the inspired word of God! We are a community, we must hold to our beliefs, and our way of life or we will fall apart. We will not survive if we waiver, if we become lukewarm.

What are we again? We are Bible believing Christians. There is evidence of our faith in this book! It is the plain word of God which all of us should be able to agree with! This is all we need to understand the world! Everything, every word in this book, is substantially true, and it shows the marvelous design of nature! It teaches us how to achieve the ideal society, to work cooperatively with one another to help our community thrive! Without every member of this congregation working towards our goal, we will choke like a flower surrounded by weeds, and die out.

And the world is full of those weeds! The world is a garden being overrun by these crawling beasts. The scriptures are the basis of our beliefs, one would think that it could create a church in which all Christians could live in a universal brotherhood under God, but is that what we see? What we see is corruption! The beast of Revelation lives and walks among us, Babylon is real! It is through the papacy we see the fulfillment of that prophecy! They and all those to whom Christ will call his enemies! Those rejected by Christ! We are not only to confess our belief in Christ, but to heartily embrace him! We are not going to be cold and primitive like the Catholic Church. We must return to plain Biblical truth and away from their fables. Christ is coming personally, so it should be personal to all people! We are God's chosen people, a new Israel, to lead the world forward. We as Americans, and Seventh Day Adventists are alone qualified for bringing salvation to the world!

It is upon us, the truth. We know that all have ever taken upon themselves the name of Christ must pass his searching scrutiny to be accepted by God! He records every move, every wasted moment, every wrong word, or selfish act, secret sin, neglectful moment. He knows. He sees your heart and your mind. Any weakening of your faith is unacceptable! God did not give us his commandments as a suggestion. He did not say, listen to these if you want, but if you don't it's alright. He demands obedience to his commandments! That's why they were given to us! They are law!

We know that the dead sleep in their graves, oblivious until the coming of Christ. Christ's atonement for our sins was incomplete, it will only be complete when he returns to judge us. We are not to rest in a state of satisfaction like many of our Protestant brothers and sisters saying "I am already saved." They believe that they only have to believe in Jesus Christ and that their faith is sufficient! Christ has not yet saved anyone. Their beliefs are only step one, once you accept his salvation, you must pay up! Your sins are not pardoned, or plotted out.

That is why we confess our sins, not to Christ, but on the head of Satan, who will carry them into oblivion with him as he is the instigator of that sin! Leviticus 16:8 says, "One lot for Jehovah, and the other lot for Azazel."

God didn't say "remember the Sabbath and keep it holy" for him to change his mind of the date. It is the seventh day of the week, not the first, that we all know. This is how we separate ourselves, the true followers, from unbelievers. This is our final test, this is how we receive the seal of approval from God. It is evidence of our true loyalty. Those who fail to do this will receive the mark of the beast, and risk losing eternal life. Thus we are here, worshipping on Saturday. Deuteronomy 5:12-13 said the Sabbath is a remembrance of her deliverance of Egypt." Exodus 31: 11-18 says, it is a sign of God's covenant with His people." Thus we read the Bible and know that God is on the eve of coming.

Daniel 8:14, "Unto 2,300 days then shall the sanctuary be cleansed." William Miller believed that was when Christ was returning to earth on October 22, 1843. He and his followers stood on roof tops, wearing their white ascension robes, fully expecting Christ to come down on the clouds in triumph. Yet they were misguided. Jesus entered to the tabernacle of holies on that day, to cleanse the temple. That means that this event has begun. The revelation is upon us, it is so close my people.

We understand that the dead are sleeping because Lazarus slept and Jesus brought him back to life, and only through his presence did that occur. The Bible says so! Ecclesiastes 9:5 states "the dead know nothing, there is no knowledge in the grave."

Matthew 27:52 says "The graves were opened and many bodies of the saints which slept arose." Only the righteous will be in New Jerusalem at the end of all of this madness in a society fully sanctified by god. This would be a summit of human achievement! So, we must work with God to transform the world from the province of Satan to the kingdom of Christ. This world, which is dominated by Satan absolutely cannot be released until the second coming. This is the final era in human history, it will be one of catastrophic tribulation augmented by a black sun and a blood red moon and war and famine. Jesus may lead a celestial army of resurrected saints and martyrs to destroy Satan and his army. Blessed is he who reads aloud the words of the prophecy. In this book we find evidence that an ordinary human has heard the voice of God and the voices of the angels and we repeat the words, "Behold, I am coming soon, blessed is he who keeps the words of the prophecy of this book." To bring this farther, it is our conviction that before the close, the gospel must be brought to every living soul. Preaching to others can bring on the end times, and that is not a bad thing. It is necessary. You must hear my words, go and spread the word. Amen."

While none of Amos Perry's words were light, this sermon seemed especially jarring. The organist began to play and my mom easily opened the hymnal pointing at "Come Thou Font." I turned my eyes to the familiar words. I knew them well enough I could sing with my eyes closed but if I wasn't looking down to the paper, my mother would knock me again.

After the service, Miss Maggie approached me and touched my arm with her cold, puffy hands. "Are you going to join us at the women's meeting?" she asked. While I loved this woman that was not something I wanted to do. My throat constricted. I hated lying in the house of God, and yet I did.

"Oliver and I have a lot of repairs to do on the chicken coop. That thunderstorm last night did a toll on it." She smiled, almost sadly, and nodded.

"Of course dear, I hope to see you there next week. I miss you." She said. She was always a warm and honest woman, and if my mother wasn't in attendance to the meeting, it wouldn't be bad, but I didn't like feeling her eyes on me now that I was able to be apart for them.

Oliver approached me, kissing my cheek. I said, "I feel like Amos was speaking directly to me."

"That's a normal feeling." he said with a smile.

Clarence and Minnie joined us and Minnie said, "I'd love to have you two come over an evening this week. I have some good news I'd like to share with you."

"I would love to," I said. "Although you're going to make me wait that long to know your good news?" I asked.

Minnie giggled lightly and nodded. "Yes, Miriam and John will be there Thursday night. Would that work for you?"

"Of course." I said.

Minnie's face became even brighter than before. "Wonderful! You and Oliver can join us after work that day. I will have something good put together for dinner."

"Do you need me to bring anything?" I asked.

"No, no, no, you're our guests."

"Alright," I said, hugging her. Her soft brown curls brushed against my cheek.

Oliver and I left in the cart for our home. The warm weather was incredibly welcome. The air felt soft with a hint of humidity, but not enough to feel oppressive and sluggish. "I did nearly everything he said not to." I said. "I ate meat, gravy, there was butter on a white roll... God above."

"You're not going to hell." He said.

"We're apparently going to go visit with the antichrist church tomorrow..." I said.

"My uncle is insane." Oliver said plainly, encouraging the horse forward. My heart sunk lightly and I felt ill. "Just because he says something doesn't make it true, Virginia."

"I've been told my entire life that he's speaking the inspired word of God."

"A lot of people think a lot of people speak the word of God. They can't all be right." Oliver said. We fell silent, and I watched the birds sitting on stone and wooden fences. Their singing put me at ease, as always. The worst part of winter was being without them. Oliver turned down the road to our beautiful white house sitting amongst the trees. Oliver helped me down and I went inside as he took the horse to the pasture. I sat down at the kitchen table and closed my eyes briefly, unsure what to think or who to listen to: my husband, or the preacher? I loved Oliver since I was young, but I was forced to listen to Perry my entire life with the assumption he knew what he was talking about. My parents believed him, so did the entire community, that was why they were going to church on Saturday.

"I thought you wanted to see what's in the trunk." He said as he walked in the door. "Just stay out here and come into the bedroom when I call you."

"You're concerning me." I breathed, stepping into the washroom and combed through my hair. I sat on the wicker basket and waited. Only a little sliver of light came in through a crystallized glass window to the right of the mirror. I held my hand up to it, and watched as the light made designs upon my skin. As the wind and clouds moved by, the forms and shapes danced.

"Virginia?" Oliver's voice was cracking and quiet.

"Yes? Can I come out now?"

"I suppose so..." he muttered. I could hardly hear him through the door. I opened it and looked out. Oliver was sitting on the bed, facing away from me, looking towards the trunk. He was wearing a dress. I stepped up to the trunk and knelt before him. He was avoiding eye contact. I could feel the tension and fear wafting off him, and how it painted his face. His hands were shaking. I took his hands in mine. "I think that you need a hat." I said. "Those dresses are supposed to be worn with hats." The amount of energy it took to respond without shock or fear was immense. My chest burned madly, the acidic feeling crawling up my throat and pouring into my stomach.

Shock crossed his face and he looked up suddenly. I went over to my part of the closet, and stood on a stepping stool to reach my sun hat. The blue flowers on it matched the flowers on that dress. I placed it on his head. He chuckled a bit. I went through the trunk. Most of the clothing was very old, some of it was even rotting away, but otherwise looked like it had been taken care of as well as it could be. "Stand up," I said, putting the clothing back in the trunk. He did so. I reached into my closet and found a dress that was always far too long for me and held it up to him. "How about that? It doesn't have holes in it. You'd probably look far prettier in it than me."

"I don't understand..." he muttered. "I thought you'd be surprised..."

"I am surprised." I responded, and crossed my arms. "I also thought we decided that there wouldn't be any judging."

"Are you judging?" he asked. "I want to know what you think."

"I've never seen a man wear a dress before, that's true." I breathed, looking at him. "Nor do I think it's normal, but if you want to and it makes you comfortable... then why not?"

"My uncle would kill me if he saw me like this."

"Well, your uncle isn't here, is he?" I said, and continued to hold the dress up in front of him. "Try it on." He nodded and started to change. "Do you go out in public like this?"

"Once or twice." he said. "Though it wasn't really public."

"I always wondered if trousers were comfortable." I said, looking at his trousers lying on the bed. I started to put them on. Although they were far too long. "These are a little constricting; don't you think?"

"Yes." Oliver said, still turned away from me. The dress I gave him was a deep green. I wasn't even sure how it managed to get into my possession. It was a little heavy along the collar but it hid that he had no chest, and covered up his Adam's apple. I slipped out of the trousers.

"I have so many questions," I said. "But I'll have to ask them while we are making dinner. French toast tonight."

"Breakfast for dinner, why?"

"I have limited cooking skills, and you have limited ingredients. That bread you have is going stale and needs to be used up."

I went into the kitchen. My mind was going in a thousand different directions, and I was only pretending like I had this all together in my head. I pulled out the skillet and put it on the stove and while it heated I cracked some eggs, added in spice and sliced the bread. Oliver stepped back out in his regular clothes. "I'm a little disappointed that you kept this from me." I breathed.

"I... I... I didn't know how to tell you." he said.

"I saw you wear your mother's pearls sometimes, that's it." I said, putting the battered bread into the skillet.

"She knew." he said. "I told her that I liked dressing like that. She gave me the pearls, actually."

I nodded and took in a deep breath. "These are things that we need to talk about now, so as to clear the air, so we don't have disagreements later concerning… well, I don't even know what it is, you wearing women's clothing, I don't know. Do you want to be a woman?" I asked.

"No," he said.

"Then why do you wear the clothing?" I asked. He was silent. "Oliver, I need to understand. Currently I don't, and it's important to me that I do."

"Because I feel better like that." he responded, standing beside the kitchen table.

"No one talked about what to do about this in the women's group… And you like men then?" I asked. "Which do you prefer? Women or men?"

I hoped it'd be an obvious question. "I… I don't know." he said. "You are the first women I've ever been with."

"Does that mean you've been with men?" I asked, my voice jumping a few octaves.

My stomach churned. "Yes."

"Oliver…"

"I don't want you to go on and on about my soul, I've been told that before…" he quietly said, almost like a beg.

"I wasn't going to," I said. "It'd just be nice if you would have mentioned that you…"

"I sure wasn't going to ask you the same question!"

"Oliver, you already knew the answer!" I pressed, flipping over the bread in the skillet. "You know everything about me, which plates I want, to what I've thought about anything and everything, and yet today I find out that I know nothing about you!"

"And I told you, you didn't!" he said, sitting down at the table, placing his head on the wood.

"I didn't expect this. I'm not angry with you, Oliver. I… I don't even know what I am about it. That's alright because it really isn't my place to tell you what you can and cannot wear or what you can and cannot do, and that goes for you with me, but somethings are just important to discuss."

"I want you to meet my friends, next week." Oliver said, some energy getting back in his voice.

"Your friends? Where at?"

"In the city." he said. "We need to get you out of Glenborough. I can call them tomorrow when you go to your father's store and we drop off the eggs to him. It's perfect!"

"Alright, as long as it doesn't entail too much excitement."

"Give it a chance, Virginia."

"I've been giving a lot of things chances lately."

I'd never been to church on a Sunday before, much less a Catholic mass, and I didn't know what to expect. Along with numerous other carts and automobiles, Oliver helped me out and I watched as many of the Irish immigrants were streaming through the large wooden doors. With all the photographs I had seen of beautiful architecture in Catholic architecture, this was crude in comparison. It was a white plaster building with two doors and a small white steeple raising into the blue sky. The bells were chiming. It was such a strong noise that I only heard from a distance before, and now it felt so strong, going through me. Oliver held my hand tightly. A man stood at the door with a smile on his face. He waved his hand at us. In a thick Irish accent he greeted Oliver and hugged him. "Virginia, this is Patrick, I work with him at the bank."

"I'm glad to finally meet you. I've heard so much." he said. He was difficult to understand, but he shook my hand fervently. "I'm excited to have visitors here, we rarely do. Come in, come in," We entered through the doors and it was quite lively. There were chunks of people within the narthex drinking what smelled like coffee. "Would you like some?" Patrick asked while he walked to the coffee pot.

"I'm sorry, I don't drink coffee." I said. Patrick nodded and took a heavy draw of it and pointed and said, "Those are my brothers. They work at the cannery. Most of the people there do."

"Wasn't that an ammunitions factory during the war?" I asked.

He nodded. "Yes, and part of it became a... what would you call it, a factory where there were seamstresses making the uniforms for the men." He took in a deep breath. "Some of our men just didn't come back, they went over to fight, so many of them." He shook his head. "Lost a brother."

"I'm sorry for your loss." I said. He nodded sadly and said, "He got to see some more of the world, though, that's what he wanted. Wanted to prove he was a good American too."

Another series of bells chimed and we entered the sanctuary. Compared to the bare open space of our church which was only lined with plain wooden pews, this was different. It was only now I saw all the beautiful stained glass windows reaching from just above the floor to the edge of the ceiling, coloring the light so exquisitely as it entered. Upon these stained glass windows were depictions of Biblical figures and events, and what I assumed to be saints. I'd heard about how Catholics revered these powerful dead people as bringers of good will, or something like that. The pews had red cushions on them. That alone was even more welcoming. Oliver and I sat beside Patrick and his family.

The priest wore a white robe with something around his neck. He looked tired, but surprisingly young. His face was fresh and dewy, unlike the rocky face of Amos. This man looked kind, if a face could betray kindness. There was a choir to his right in some other pews, also wearing strange long garments. In a way I could see how Amos saw them primitive, especially when the service began by the man speaking in another language. It wasn't like the strange individual bursting out, speaking in tongues, he was speaking Latin. I couldn't follow, and the hymnal only helped a little bit in deciphering the language, but already no one was yelling at me.

The liturgy was oddly calming. It had purpose and history, and I could feel that. The entire church felt warm. The people weren't bursting out with their hands in their air in fits of hysteria that occasionally happened in our church. One could say these people were stoically saying words they had memorized as children, and following rituals, they were, but many of them were still doing so fervently, and with belief. Upon the choir beginning, the strangest feeling wafted over me. It was almost trance like. The most beautiful sound I had ever encountered came into my ears, and flooded my veins.

As the choral music continued, the sound of human voices became nearly angelic. I'd never experienced something so spiritual in my life, not in my own church, not anywhere. To bring myself back to the plane of the living, I clutched Oliver's hand tightly. He kissed it, and yet my heart stayed with the choral music. I was disappointed when it ended. I let out a heavy breath in relief. The priest began his sermon. His voice was smooth, calm, and intelligent. He didn't bellow out fire and brimstone. He only simply thanked his congregation for their sacrifices in the war which only ended in November of the previous year, and how they were a light upon the earth.

Near a classroom outside the narthex of the church was a wall with the faces of the church members who died. Some of the photographs were of the men with their families, or their service photographs. Family and friends attached notes to the photographs and wall, and below it were some vases with fresh flowers. I approached the wall while Oliver spoke to his coworker. The noise of the accented voices filled the air like static and the sound of massive amounts of coffee being poured into cups gave a smoother noise to the clamor. The clanking of ceramic cups and the rush of water from the sink began in earnest as the last few people left the sanctuary. It was strange to look into the eyes of these dead men who probably died, terrified, in the trenches, gulping poison gas or with a bullet to their head. They looked so peaceful in these photographs, at ease, almost unreal.

On Thursday that week, Clarence drove Oliver and I to his house, on the other side of town from Mother and Father. Clarence was silent with a smile on his face, like he was trying to keep a secret. Oliver held my hand tightly. He acted strangely since Saturday when he told me his own secret. In a way, I tried to pretend like nothing changed even though he freely wore his mother's pearls in the house, and occasionally a dress. I pretend like all was well when I knew this was not alright. He was a deviant, or an invert as my mother would call him. Perry would call him a pervert. If anyone found out… I couldn't even imagine. I was scared for him, and for myself I well. I married someone I knew nothing about, when I thought I married him for safety because I trusted him, and now I felt like I knew very little.

Oliver and I were welcomed inside by Minnie whose face was flushed with joy. She hugged us both and said, "Would you like some water? It's getting pretty warm out there today. It's just so nice out, though, I have all the windows open and the drapes pulled back. It lets in all the sun, but it heats the place up…" She rambled on, moving to the kitchen at a quick pace. Her words were so sudden that I didn't react immediately. "Yes, please, Minnie." Oliver said.

She giggled a bit and said, "Virginia, you've really got yourself a gentleman."

Clarence walked in and hung his hat on the coat rack near the door. "Do you want to tell them?" Clarence asked.

"Yes, yes," she said, walking up to Clarence and taking his hand. "You know about my sister, of course," she began. "She left five children behind. Many of which my mother took in, but because she can't take care of all of them, Clarence and I decided to adopt her youngest, Joy. She's taking a bit of a nap now in her room." Minnie's face lit up. "It's like having my sister back in the house, she's just like her."

"That's extraordinary." I said. "You must be so happy."

"We are," Minnie said, hugging Clarence's arm tighter.

"You're legally adopting her?" I asked.

"Yes, we are going through the rest of the paperwork. She's going to be ours. I'll go check up on her to see if she's up." She went down the wooden clad hallway. Clarence sat down on the armchair and pulled his hair back with his hand.

"I almost thought you'd never have children. You've been married for nearly three years."

"That's not that long." he said with a chuckle. "Minnie didn't know if she wanted to have her own children because of the... the bad history in her family. There's always been so many pregnancy complications." He peered back towards the hallway. Minnie walked over with the girl beside her. They were holding hands and the girl yawned.

Minnie knelt down next to Joy and said, "Joy, this is your aunt and uncle, Virginia and Oliver." She waved a bit. She couldn't have been over six years old. "Will you say hello to them?"

"Hello," she said.

"Are you hungry for dinner?" she asked the little girl. She nodded again. With all the stories I heard of Minnie's sister, I didn't expect the girl to be so quiet or shy. When we sat down at the table, Minnie brought out an egg tart with a large loaf of bread. She beamed with pride and stood at the head of the table with her hands around the top of the chair. "How does it look, Virginia? You're a better cook than I."

"Better cook? This looks wonderful, Minnie." I said, smiling. It really did look delicious, and I was hungry. It was getting to the point I was always hungry for just about anything rich.

"Clarence, would you do the prayer?" she asked. She showed Joy how to fold her hands together and bow her head. We all followed in her lead.

"Come lord Jesus be our guest, at this table let us be blessed. Amen." It was the basic prayer given by my mother and father every meal of our life.

It was beautiful to see Clarence in the family he always wanted. There was such peace on his face. It was soothing to me as well. Minnie and Clarence continued to make eye contact with one another, touching one another's hands. Minnie also had a piece of her sister with her forever, and a child of her own. In a way, I wanted something like that. I wanted children. The atmosphere in the air with a child around was so light. I wanted that in my home.

Chapter Six

Oliver and I prepared for bed that night. I sat in front of the mirror, pulling the beautiful comb through my hair. Oliver straightened out the bed, flattening the sheets, putting that day's newspaper in an organized pile under the bed. I washed my face with cold water before sitting beside him on the cool, crisp sheets freshly taken from the drying line. I placed my head on his shoulder and kissed the small patch of skin. He lowered his head and kissed my forehead. "What's on your mind?" he asked. "You're thinking awful hard about something."

"I want a family." I said. He took in a deep breath and froze for a moment. "You don't?"

"I didn't say that, Virginia. I don't know if we're ready yet."

"You don't think so?" I asked quietly. I kissed his cheek, and turned his head toward mine so my lips rested on his.

"I don't," he breathed, pulling away slightly, making eye contact. "I'm not any good to be a father."

"I don't believe that." I said, kissing him again. He sighed and leaned over me and kissed me back, his hand resting on the sleeve of my nightgown, pushing away the soft white cotton. "I love you," I said.

Friday night came around and Oliver's plans were coming to fruition, and I patiently awaited what was coming to me, whether that was going to be a terrifying experience or not. I promised him I'd be willing to try all sorts of new things. "Good night, Clarence!" Oliver called as we exited the general store, a cloud of flour trailing behind me as I left. Clarence waved back at me with a smile on his face. He said all was well at his house with Joy and Minnie. They were constructing a new reality. "Remember? I arranged for you to meet my friends. They are coming by tonight to pick us up in their automobile!"

"I haven't forgotten anything." I breathed, some heat entering my chest. Fear was one thing, and apprehension was another, and possibly a combination of the two was what was going on in my body. "I've never been in one of those." I said, my face breaking into a smile. "I should get freshened up then! I'm covered in flour. I'm always covered in flour…" I patted my sleeves and watched the clouds of flour rise and get carried off by the wind. We turned the cart beside the house. He helped me down before hurrying to take the horse out to the pasture. I stepped inside and lit the lamps before bringing out a nice dress of mine. I looked at it for a minute, wondering if it was proper enough.

Oliver jogged in. "I think that you should wear that red dress of yours, and I should make a few alterations before we leave."

"The red one?" I asked, lifting it up. "It's a little small,"

"It's a little tight." he answered. "Do you want to fit in where we are going?" I nodded. "Alright, then, put that on."

"Are you wearing… that green dress?" I asked, my voice cracking a bit.

"If you don't mind." he said, looking me in the eye. He honestly sounded excited. I nodded. "Then I will." He took in a deep breath and we both dressed in silence. He looked quite pretty in the green dress. It fit his bodily well. He put

60

his mother's pearls around his neck. "Can you stand on the step stool?" he asked. I stepped up, my head above his now. He touched my cheek briefly before he rustled through my sewing kit in the closet. When he returned to the stool he said, "Don't move, stay still." I stood there and he began to cut off the bottom of my dress with my good cloth shears.

"What are you doing Oliver?" I asked, terror running through me. "This is a nice dress!"

"I'm making it so you fit in. Make sure you wear your black stockings to cover up all that hair on your legs unless you plan to shave them." he said bluntly.

"You are acting very rudely." I stated.

"You will see why I'm doing this later, Ginny, just trust me now." he breathed. I sat down, wondering why the hem of my dress was now raised above my ankles. He cut so evenly that there were no frays or unevenness. I didn't know he was skilled like that. I pulled my black stockings up as far as they went, but they barely went over my knees. Oliver sat in front of one of the mirrors with the lamp right beside him. He opened a carved cherry box from beside him and lifted out a sculpted head with a wig atop it. He began to comb the hair out.

"Are you going to wear that?" I asked, trying to keep my voice even.

He nodded. "Yes. My mother also gave me this." He lifted it from the head and placed it on his own. The hair was bobbed, and about the color of his natural hair, a deep chestnut. He formed it around his face and looked in the mirror. Within the desk, he sat at was a drawer I'd never opened. From this shallow drawer was a golden case. He was going to wear lipstick.

"Where did you get that?" I asked rushing to the desk. "We aren't supposed to wear cosmetics."

"I'm not supposed to be wearing a dress, or pearls." he quietly replied. "Would you like to try it? I promise you, you won't be damned for all eternity for wearing lipstick." He handed it to me. It was a creamy rose color. I very carefully did exactly as he had. "Perfect." I continued to get glimpses of myself in the mirror. We both looked so different. For a moment there I thought: my husband is a woman.

Chapter Seven

Not entirely a woman of course, he still had that skinned rabbit of his, but the way he was now, it was difficult to remember that was there. We stood near the door way, both dolled up probably more extravagantly than we were at our wedding, waiting. All I needed was flowers in my hair. "If your voice is going to change, I'm going to need a warning." I said bluntly.

"It's not going to change." he sighed, placing his hand on my back. The automobile pulled up, lights at the front practically blinding Oliver and I. The man stepped out from behind the wheel very abruptly and stepped up to us. "Oliver," he said with a smile. "And this must be Virginia. It's very nice to meet you; my name is George."

"Hello George." I said with a little bit of a laugh. He kissed my hand. He was dolled up in a nice grey suit with a colorful boater hat. He motioned to the car and there we got in. It felt so strange sitting on such soft seats but with the motor beneath us. The chair vibrated underneath of me. It was very unnatural feeling, and not at all safe. The car puttered quite a bit, but was far faster and more reliable than a horse once it started moving. This didn't have a mind of its own. "Virginia, this is my wife Clara."

"Hello, Clara." I said. She looked back to me and smiled.

"I'm glad to see Oliver is being himself tonight. We have not been able to see him in quite a while; he's been too busy preparing for you to come." I didn't quite know if her voice was light or not. She might not have liked me.

Oliver fell quiet. He put his hands on his lap just like I did at church, and sat with his ankles crossed, just like Mother kept trying to get me to do, but I always forgot. His breathing was shallower and controlled, but even, like he had transformed into a very proper woman. His back was straight and his neck looked graceful. The green dress really did cover up his Adam's apple and his flat chest. I took a hold of his hand in mine for some comfort. My stomach was crawling with just being in the automobile. Any dips in the road were rough and made my stomach bounce on the inside.

"How did the wedding go, you two?" George asked.

"Swimmingly." Oliver stated.

"You can't swim." George said with a sigh.

"I thought you said you'd learn," I gleefully laughed.

"I never got to it I guess. Being an adult has interfered with learning how to swim. That doesn't mean it didn't go well George, I just had a poor choice in words. It was very pleasant."

"I was a bit overwhelmed with all the people." I said. "Miss Maggie kept it very much under control."

"I love that old woman." Clara said. "You know she is my mother's great-great aunt. I don't really know what that means, but it's nice to know there are some long living folk in my family, that way they don't all croak by the time they get to forty like they tend to. We have a lot of living to do, don't we George?"

"Get to it as much as we can!" he exclaimed.

"I'm bringing Virginia out here to have fun. She doesn't know what fun is." Oliver said heatedly.

Clara looked back to me. "Don't know how to have fun? That's a shame. You will soon! It's not that scary."

We were driving into the busy city. I'd only been here once or twice with Father to pick up some orders, but now that we had them all delivered to us, I didn't have need to be around such congested streets that were being filled with people and horses and other cars. "How did you get yourselves a car?" I asked.

George and Clara looked to each other for a moment. "We have a very lucrative business."

"What is it, may I ask?"

"You will see in just a moment." We pulled up to the flashing lights of a hotel called The Brigadier Angel.

"You own a hotel?" I asked in amazement. "That is magnificent, it looks beautiful even from the outside. How did you meet Oliver over here then?"

"He's our banker." George said. "Helps us run our finances. All of them. Please, come inside." A man opened the door for us wearing a nice suit and he tipped his hat to Clara, Oliver, and I. There was a golden chandelier hanging from the ceiling, sparkling with so much light which dashed itself against the plush carpeted surface beneath my feet. Quite honestly, I wanted to take my stockings right off, despite my hairy legs, so my toes could feel the scarlet softness. We were not waiting in the lobby long. Clara and George, who locked arms were walking to the right, past large golden framed picture windows. This place looked like it belonged to royalty. Everything I saw looked too expensive to touch: every painting, every sculpture, vase, plant even. Oliver's body language didn't change when we walked in, giving me the impression that he'd been here before, if not many times.

There was a room numbered 080. Clara very gently opened the door and peered in before the door was opened to allow the rest of us in. Then George very quickly closed the door behind us. The room was not a hotel room like I thought it'd be. Instead there was another door directly behind it that led to a well-lit staircase lined by false torches on the wall. "Where are we going?" I whispered to Oliver.

Noise wafted up from the stone staircase. Laughter and music, the pattering of feet and clanging of dishes and glasses grew with each step we took. "You'll see. You're never very patient, are you?" he whispered.

We entered into a large ballroom space. It didn't match my expectations of a fairytale like those my mother used to read to Miriam and I. There was a band up front, with a black lady wearing sparkling silver, singing her heart out. The rest of the floor was in chaos with writhing bodies. There were women wearing short dresses with short hair that had been dyed black. There was alcohol everywhere. The smell was pungent and mixed with fragrant perfume. We'd been told from a very young age the evils of alcohol, we were never to drink it, we weren't supposed to dance or enjoy music like this… yet Oliver very quickly took my hand and we began to sway back and forth to the rhythm of the music. My brain stopped working for a moment. There was such a smile on his face, while I was concerned that my face betrayed a very different emotion. As I looked around, though, there were many other people like him and I here. There were women wearing trousers, there were men in dresses. Almost everyone had cosmetics painting their faces, and all of them were drinking. As a waiter came back carrying a tray, Oliver slipped one of the half empty glasses from it. "Try it," he said with a smile.

"I'm not supposed to." I said.

"This, just like makeup, is not going to land you in hell for all eternity, Ginny." he lightly responded, leaning towards me to kiss my ear. I took a hold of the glass and took a swig, immediately disgusted by the burning, putrid sensation in my mouth. I coughed. "A little strong for you maybe?" Oliver laughed and patted my back, downing the rest in one gulp. "A soda might be better for you."

He flitted over towards another waiter and took a glass from them as well. I took it and sipped from it, just as startled by this but not as disgusted. There was no burning, but there was buzzing with the substance. It was pleasant and even refreshing. Oliver smiled and after I finished my drink, we returned to the dance floor. He was twirling in the green dress, acting unlike I had ever seen him in my life, which may have been a lie. If I knew what was in his heart, I could have pieced this together much earlier. In either case, I still found myself with my arms around him and my head resting on his chest, listening to his heart with the music. I was in love and I felt safe in his arms, safer than I'd ever felt before. It was a different kind of safety than that of being secured in a location without danger. It was that of being at ease, completely, even in such a strange, and foreign environment.

Nonetheless, I was never a fan of enormous groups of people. My energy was being drained from me swiftly. I analyzed everything to get a sense of the location; the brass players on stage with their shining instruments, the bassist in the back that was far smaller than the instrument he played, and the woman in the front whose kind I'd never seen in person before. She sang just like an angel, but with more depth and passion. She probably had more to sing for than an angel.

Clara and George were enjoying their night too. Clara calmly watched the performers while George was standing behind her with his arms around her, and she held his arms with her slender, long hands. They were totally at ease and in perfect harmony. He rested his chin on her head and there was a calm, nice smile painted on his face. I understood them in a way. Their life was far different than what I was used to. Such glamor was not something I was ever allowed into before. I'd been told life was only to prepare the earth for the second coming of Christ. These people were just living for the sake of living. It was far less complicated and far less scary.

If I lived like them, I wouldn't have to fear dying without living at all.

Upon arriving home, I was exhausted and wanted nothing more than sleep. The bed looked so welcoming. I walked into the room, and slid my shoes off, kicking them into the closet and sat down at the desk turned vanity. Oliver stood behind me, one hand on each shoulder. "Ever curious about what it'd be like to kiss a woman?"

"I'm still getting used to kissing men." I said, wiping my lipstick off. I looked back to him and despite all that was on him I said, "You're still a man."

He sat down on the edge of my trunk and carefully removed the wig. "Are you prepared to hear tomorrow that everything we did was worthy of being damned?" he asked.

"You truly hate going to church, don't you?" I said.

"It's not my favorite thing to do with my time…" he said with a sigh. "I lived with Amos long enough that I've had my fill of sermons for a life time."

He got into his pajamas at sat on his side of the bed. "You are still going tomorrow. People will ask questions if you don't." I said.

"I will, but eventually you need to learn to lie."

Chapter Eight

"For we all know what John says: for an hour is coming when all who are in the tombs will hear His voice. Daniel replies by saying many of those who sleep in the dust of the earth shall awake, some to everlasting life, and some to shame and everlasting judgment." Reverend Perry's voice blasted through the congregation sitting neatly in rows of uncomfortable wooden pews. Oliver was on my left, and my Father was on my right. My mother wasn't near enough to me that she could smack me for slouching just a bit, but I wasn't slouching. "For the evildoers shall be cut off, but those who wait in the Lord shall inherit the land! In just a little while, the wicked will be no more; though you will look carefully at this place, He will not be there. But the meek shall inherit the land, and delight themselves in abundant peace."

Amos stepped out from behind his pulpit and stood in the center of the aisle. "Behold, all souls are mine, sayeth the Lord; the soul of the father as well as the soul of the son. Is your name in the book of life? Are worthy to have it written there! Will you be the ones inheriting the earth, or shall you perish forever? Our cause is written for us by Matthew: Behold I am sending you out as sheep in the midst of wolves, so be wise as serpents and innocent as doves. We are trusted with the task of changing the world. As Isaiah says He shall judge between nations and shall decide disputes for many peoples; and they shall beat their swords into plowshares, and their spears into pruning hooks; nation shall not lift up sword against nation, neither shall they learn war anymore." Amos's voice fell and he took in a deep breath. "Just imagine… a world without war, without our young men leaving to die on a battle field, not remembering what hope, or beauty was anymore, not seeing their faith come to fruition with blood on their hands. Imagine that we can stop all of this; that we as people can live in peace. As we speak, those in this room, all of you live comfortably in your homes. You sit here without fear of persecution for your beliefs or of not getting your next meal, nor do you fear that you will be shot in cold blood in the streets, nor that you will be robbed of your livelihood. We are those who have chosen the path to avoid such circumstances; there are those in the towns and cities who are not so lucky. They are wracked by disease and poverty. We can assist. We have the means, and the opportunity to do so. Only do we need to get up off of our couches and spend some time on the people who have never had others give their time to them."

Amos's voice was now hardly above a whisper. When he nodded we knew he was finished. "I have signups in the narthex for such activities that will be catered to this week, please take a look at them."

We sung a single hymn following his short, and simple tirade: "Be thou my vision". As we stood up I whispered to Oliver, "I don't feel as innocent as a dove."

"You're a dove." he responded, kissing my cheek.

The activities for this week were very interesting, but there was little I was qualified for doing except for making meals for the homeless in the nearby town which would be served at the

Brigadier Angel Hotel. I was already familiar with the location now. Oliver and I looked at each other with smiles pasted on our cheeks, and I wrote our names down. It was still very odd seeing Oliver and Virginia Crain. I refused to write down Mr. and Mrs. Oliver Crain because my name was not Oliver. It was still Virginia. It looked like Wednesday evening I'd have to have something prepared to deliver to the Brigadier.

That seemed to be how our weeks worked. We had a very good system arranged. This week and for a good chunk of time afterwards Wednesday's were the time we'd go to prepare and serve meals to the homeless and the impoverished, which was at first, a little scary, but after speaking with the people taking the meals, it was fascinating. All the food we brought was eaten and appreciated. On Friday's, mostly, Oliver and I would meet up with Clara and George and go to the hotel. Each week it was different, sometimes it'd be as it was the first time, drinking and dancing with a live band, and at other times there would be a fancy dinner, or a magician, or a concert. Oliver was paying for it all, and I didn't know where the money was from. He did take care of our personal finances, as I took care of the store's, but I told myself not to be concerned. I was learning to genuinely enjoy life, even if it went against my instincts and beliefs. There wasn't a little voice in my heart telling me to stop, instead it was my stomach being afraid of what my mother would say if she found out.

Reverend Perry took on a new crusade, the temperance movement. It was clear we weren't supposed to drink, but he hardly mentioned it in great detail about the rest of the world not doing it either, but the long drawn out sermons about the evils of drinking and the culture surrounding it made me very uncomfortable as I had tried drinking alcohol on a few occasions. Although I didn't find it very good and actually disgusting and unnecessary, that didn't mean that Oliver abstained from it. He only drank when we went out, and for that I was thankful. Perry said that there were men coming home every day drunk and nearly passed out because of the drink. I tried to convince myself, though, that Amos was not the authority on all things in our religion, but it was difficult to convince myself otherwise. My entire life I looked at him as the leader who knew all things, who I should trust, but everything felt wrong. He was too zealous for me. In any case though, Oliver and I were still in that pew every Saturday as to avoid gossip. It kept my mother happy which in turn made everything else in life easier.

She thought I finally assimilated completely into the simple culture she wanted for me, and I was beginning to truly think that the simple might be nice just so this fear and jumpiness wouldn't be in my heart, but then I also wouldn't feel joy as much nor the energy and laughter. I wouldn't dance. I liked to dance and spin and twirl… and feel. Up until my marriage the only things I felt were the sun on my face and the grass beneath me, and the wind, and the rain, and the cold, and flour on my lips and skin. Exhilaration and adrenaline was virtually unknown. Although all these feelings felt dangerous they also felt important, natural feelings, meaning they were supposed to be in my body, ordained by God as much as any other demurer emotion, or experience.

Oliver too kept on wearing those dresses, following the same line of thought. They were wants from the heart; thus they must be ok. But he only wore the dress when we went out. I was married to three different Oliver's, honestly, the one I saw at home when it was only me and him, the one I saw at church, and the woman I saw outside of the home while we were out and about, and each Oliver was different.

One was smiley, human, alive. The other was quiet, proper, subdued. The last was still foreign to me: the other was a dress and makeup wearing, dancing, drinking, woman, man hybrid type thing who was very interested in sex. I wasn't really sure how else to characterize him, or her.

A few weeks later I was standing outside in the warm breeze. It was mid-summer now. The locusts were buzzing in the trees, making a constant, comforting ringing in my ears. The wind was hot, but fresh. The trees were telling me that it was going to rain. The leaves turned over with the pressure in the air. High above were darkening clouds, but for now the sun was golden and pushing through to the ground in steady, strong rays that colored the fields between this home, and my Father's home.

The chickens were walking about the yard, pecking at the ground. I tossed grain to them, much to their pleasure. One of the barn cats walked up, meowing. I bent down to pet her. She had a few little kittens following her, all fluffy and happily sniffing the ground. I went inside and cracked a few of the eggs and mixed it with bits of bread and gave it to them. They curled around the bowl and happily licked the concoction up.

Birds flew close ahead, sending the chickens running for their coop. I sat beneath a tree and watched as the horses in the pasture land chased after one another, their feet beating the ground in steady thumps. They tossed their heads in the breeze, their manes picked up the air. Standing near the edge of the barbed wire fence were some goats whose milk we'd use in the baked goods, and cashmere I'd sell in the general store. I had visions of gaining a following for the extra soft wool, but I had to wait an entire season, until spring, to gather wool to sell. The goats were gathered together near an outcrop of rocks, climbing them, nagging at each other. With one good leap they'd be able to get right out of the pasture, but they seemed happily occupied. There were a few younger ones, kids, hopping about, and head-butting one another.

I heard the cart moving up and turned to see Oliver moving in towards the barn with the fourth horse of ours. He waved at me, and there was a big smile on his face. I stood up from beneath the tree and waited for him to unhook the cart and let the horse loose with its friends. He put an arm on my shoulder and said, "I have something for you."

"You do?" I asked with a smile. "Dinner is cooking."

We came inside and I sat down at the kitchen table. He leaned against the table and handed me a box. "Open it, Ginny." he said, beaming brightly.

The box was heavy, cased in what looked like leather. I opened it and there was a strange looking wristwatch, handmade, and dotted with metal. "It's extraordinary." I said, pulling it out of the box, looking at the little hand ticking on perfectly.

"This was given to me as a gift for you by a friend of mine. He wants us to come by his house for dinner on Saturday." Oliver took the wristwatch and fastened it on me.

"Another friend of yours I haven't met?" I asked.

"He was in the war, actually just came back recently. He just stopped by the bank today." Oliver noted.

"That sounds like some good fun." I said, hugging him. "Why has it taken him so long to speak with you?"

"He just came in from New York actually. Before the war, he was studying there at Columbia University." Oliver proceeded to speak more about his day at the bank, which didn't include much. We had a vegetable stew to eat and some fresh bread from the store. We joked about the smallest things, mo-

ments which made me very happy that we were able to live together. I loved being able to see him so much. I felt completely
at ease for a moment.

That night while we were preparing for bed, it was taking
Oliver some time to slip into his trousers, looking at himself in
the mirror. "You seem to be quite happy with yourself." I said
with a laugh, sitting at the vanity, combing out my hair by the
light of the lantern. It was pretty much black outside by now.

"Well, why not?"

"Did you name that thing of yours or something? Like
Albert. Looks like an Albert to me. Albert is a rabbit's name."
All I got in response was a sigh a small smirk.

Saturday came with surprising haste. With each passing
week, was how much faster time went on with age. Days didn't
seem like an eternity, but a slow blink. I was sure that when I
got older, they'd become faster blinks. Oliver wasn't wearing
his green dress, or the wig, or the pearls when we went out. He
just wore his church clothes and his favorite hat. "Can I wear
your pearls?" I asked.

He smirked a bit. "Can I trust you with them?"

"I hope that's sarcasm." I muttered. "Hand them over.
You said you wanted us to look presentable."

"I didn't mean it... badly," he pressed, bringing out the
velvet lined box he kept the pearls in. He was so protective of
them.

"What did you mean by that anyways? Am I not always
presentable?"

"Not when you're covered in flour, or when you wake up
in the morning." He stood behind me and took a hold of my
hair gently and combed through it.

"And how bad could I possibly be in the morning?" I
asked. "Especially in comparison to you."

"Your hair." he said. "It's a rat's nest in the morning."

"And are you going to fix that now?" I asked, cocking my head to the side. He began to braid my hair, almost as skilled as my sister Miriam was at the task. The braid went all the way around my head and was tucked neatly in the back of my head.

"Perfect." he said. I opened up his golden cosmetics case and put the lipstick on. "We need to go to the city to get some more. I'm running low."

"Cosmetics?"

"I know where they sell Maybelline, but I shouldn't buy it." he breathed, kissing my cheek.

I nodded. "Is that what we are going to do today after meeting this mystery friend of yours?"

"He could take us to a department store. Have you ever been to one of those?" he asked, sitting down next to me. I was powdering my face with the fresh smelling soft fluffy thing that he kept in the case with other such things. I shook my head. I wasn't sure what it did, but it felt nice.

"What's this?" I asked, holding up a black tube.

"Mascara, it makes your eye lashes bigger."

"Why would you need to have bigger eyelashes?" I asked, opening it. There was a brush attached to a small tube inside the bigger tube and it was covered in black sludge.

"Turn towards me. We can try it on you." He took a hold of the tube. "Keep your eyes open, alright?" He very carefully put the mascara on my eye lashes. It felt cold and slightly heavy. "Look in the mirror."

It did look rather nice, not nearly as horrible as the picture in my head was. I blinked some and said, "Interesting."

"You think so?" he said with a smile. It still startled me that my husband new how to put cosmetics on better than I.

It was still early in the morning when we left on the bumpy cart. I was wrapped up in my shawl as we bounced through town, past the church and onto a rural road. It was empty, lined only by some livestock, and beyond that: wilderness. The forest surrounding us was beautiful, but relatively untouched. The closely collected pines stretched up to the blue, cloudy sky. They formed a strong wall against the developed world. Just outside the city, we followed an ancient cobble road which passed through high iron gates and to a colonial era house made of brick, complete with two stories and a well-tended garden of shrubbery and fruit trees and thick, dark ivy. The entire place was alive, and green, and fragrant. Large flower gardens spread alongside the driveway, alive with late summer blooms. Oliver helped me down and just then front door opened. The friend stepped out and smiled calmly. "You finally came Oliver!" the man called. Oliver unhitched the horses and gave them a long rein.

We stepped up to the man who shook Oliver's hand cordially. "This is my wife, Virginia." Oliver said.

"She's just as gorgeous as you described." the man said, smiling, touching my chin. If Oliver didn't trust him so much, I'd smack his hand away from my face. His nearness was simply uncomfortable, as was his unwavering eye contact. "It is nice to meet you, I'm Albert." I could feel Oliver almost laugh. "Am I missing something?" he asked.

"No, no, I apologize, it's very nice to meet you as well." I added.

"Please, come inside my home. I have some breakfast prepared." His voice was very proper and cold. I'd never met a person with his countenance before. We passed through a brightly lit passage and into a warm, plush study greeting us immediately to the left. Outside of the study was a large, intimidating wooden staircase stretching up into the second story which was unlit and unseeable. To the right of the staircase was a partially lit formal living room that looked like it'd been untouched for years and in pristine condition. Any step on that carpet and I'd feel guilty for ruining the perfection.

Just as Albert promised, breakfast was served on silver platters and cups. "Please sit, my home is just as much mine as it is yours." His hands were outstretched as he stood in the center of the study door.

"Thank you," I breathed. Oliver melted into the red velvety couch comfortably and I sat beside him, my back as straight as Mother would have wanted. I reverted to all my mother's teachings. I wasn't comfortable in the least. This place looked unreal and part of a mysterious old world. "So Albert, how did you and Oliver meet?" I asked.

Albert was pouring himself some tea. "I have an absolutely terrible memory, although I think it was when I was walking in the city, and Oliver almost ran me over with his rickety bicycle."

Oliver nodded, cracking into a chuckle. "Yes, that's right! I was making a delivery for… for I think it was your father actually, Ginny, and I was on my way back, and I guess I wasn't looking…" He looked at his own cup and kept on chuckling. "I broke Albert's arm actually. I took him to the hospital."

"Oliver said that you went to Columbia University, what did you study?" I asked, feeling like Oliver wasn't going to continue with his story.

"History. I was interrupted by the war and sent to France instead."

"What was it like to fight in the war?" I asked, pouring myself some tea.

"It's like expecting to be dead any moment. It was so confusing, being amongst so many different worlds. A cavalry can't fight against machine guns and tanks and air planes, nor can humans hardly deal with all the poison gas. There was just digging into the ground and waiting it out in trenches, thinking that you'd become part of the dirt soon enough. It was hell. I wasn't expecting the live until the next day, and yet I did."

"It was hell coming to earth." I said calmly, my voice just a whisper.

"Hell coming to earth? In what way do you mean?" His voice too was calm, but questioning.

"The world is coming to an end, clearly." I said. "You know of the world events; you've even been part of it. What else is happening?"

"Well, Russia is having a revolution and becoming communist... they overturned the czar and their autocracy, and Germany is in ruins... America is no longer isolationist, but becoming a world policeman. However, this is no more the end of the world than any other time in history."

"I apologize; my wife is Adventist." Oliver interjected with a sigh.

"Meaning that since the mid 1800's your group of people has thought the world was very soon coming to an end?" I nodded in agreement. "The Great Disappointment was over sixty years ago, wasn't it? The world is still turning on as before."

"That event was a misunderstanding. With all this chaos though, the changes... can't you not see it?" I asked, feeling my heart beat quickly.

"You must also believe that dancing can lead to the end of civilization as well." he said.

"Excuse me?"

"And that music must undermine your morality."

"I have a feeling that you are mocking my faith, however, I must say the signs are quite obvious that there is serious change coming…"

Albert set his cup down and made himself more comfortable on his frilly chair. "What do you think the European people thought in the 1300's when there was famine that wiped out 15% of the population, and then the Black Death which took out half of what was remaining and then numerous revolts spanning the entirety of Europe? Was that not apocalypse enough for them? The world has since turned on. Didn't the people in Germany think the world was ending when the Reformation happened and people started to turn against their traditional faith, and there was bloody war for a hundred years? There are so many events that dot history that are far worse than the situation we are in today. We don't understand fear in comparison, nor war, nor death. Even though Europe is in ruinsh, they will rebuild and do it all over again probably. I'm sure that in a hundred years, the world will look quite different, but it will still be turning and existing, and your people will still sit in their churches declaring that the world will still be ending due to different chaotic situations that arise." He sat with his elbows on his knees, maintaining eye contact.

I looked down to the tea and quietly said, "Faith is faith nonetheless." There was nothing else to say.

"And I suppose I have nothing to say against that, specifically." Albert said. "As you said, faith is faith, it is like looking at a dark staircase and guessing what is at the top, without knowing what is actually there."

"And it doesn't mean I'm wrong." I hissed.

"Alright, it's getting a little tense in this room, and I don't do tense very well." Oliver said nervously. He stood up and went over to the radio. "How about some music, and we can relax for a little while."

"No, I have some questions." I said sternly. Oliver looked over to me, startled, and didn't touch the radio.

"Yes?"

"For both of you." I took in a deep breath, trying to pull all my courage together. This may be the only opportunity to ask these questions. "Oliver, you told me that I was the first woman you had ever been with, implying that you had been with a man. Is Albert that man?" I sounded as collected as I could despite the subject of my sentence, and waited patiently while the two looked at each other uncomfortably.

"Yes." he finally said. I tried to push the visuals out of my mind as I didn't understand how that would work at all, and I didn't particularly want to know. Oliver walked back over to his chair and stood with his hands clutching the back.

"And did you bring me here for a reason? Did you want to… continue to see him?" My voice fell to hardly above a breath. That was the only thought that pervaded my mind, that he wanted a man more than he wanted me.

The two looked at each other again. Oliver moved to sit down beside me, not putting any weight hardly on the cushion, as tense as he was. "I hadn't thought of it, honestly…" Oliver mumbled.

"But you'd consider it?" I asked.

Albert said, "Let me interrupt. I have just taken up a professorship. Due to the… delicacy of the situation, and that if it was known by the board that I am a homosexual, I would mostly likely lose my position before I even start. It is best, for now, not to continue the relationship." Oliver took in a deep breath, as if relieved.

"Are you angry, Ginny?" Oliver asked.

"Am I angry? Am I not allowed to be angry? I come here to meet a man you once had a romantic relationship with, and you never bothered to tell me before we got married and then this man goes on mocking my faith? What is the meaning of this?" I stood up and moved towards the door.

Oliver jumped up and took a hold of my sleeve. "Ginny, please,"

"Please what? Honestly, I'd like to leave now." I said, crossing my arms. Albert stood up from his chair and had his hands in his pockets. He didn't appear like he was affected at all by my words.

Albert nodded to us and Oliver and I left. "Why did you bring me to this man?"

"He wanted to meet you." Oliver quietly said.

"For what purpose?" I asked, pulling the wristwatch off. "You can have this back. I don't need a reminder that my husband would rather be with such a rude, godless man."

Chapter Nine

"Would it help to go to that department store?" Oliver asked, his voice hardly above a whisper now. "We could eat at a really nice place, maybe explore a bit." I shrugged. "I'm just going to tell myself that's a yes…" Oliver turned onto the main road that led into town. The houses were becoming closer and closer together. The place smelled like it was rotting. Yet as we went on, the homes became bigger and cleaner, made of stone rather than wood, and had nice doors and windows rather than just curtains or panels. On the corner of the city at an intersection that was filled with automobiles and carts and taxis as well, was the department store. It was many stories high, and looked extraordinary, and intimidating as well. So many of these new things were intimidating due to their size, stature, and what they stood for. This was the emporium of all things commercial, things that I wasn't supposed to waste my time, money and energy on, and yet here Oliver and I were, standing at the door, about to walk in, looking like we fit in surprisingly well.

The expansive building had all sorts of electric lights hanging from the ceiling, and there were many people milling about wearing hats and furs and other things that didn't match with summer weather. There were kitchen supplies, and clothing, and bedding, almost anything imaginable. "Over here," Oliver said, linking arms with me. We walked with false dignity. He walked and acted like a man although we were here to buy cosmetics for him. There was a brightly lit area with women who worked for the store, spraying perfumes. There were light floral smells and heavy musks that made me want to cough, and we had to go through them to reach cosmetics counter. Oliver stood back, allowing me to look at the wonders that were being watched closely by the lady behind the counter. I was wearing makeup right now, I looked like I belonged. I looked for a lipstick that matched Oliver's, but there other types like lip stains and flavored ones and creams… I didn't know if he wanted the same thing or something different. "Which do you like, Oliver?" I asked, motioning for him to come over.

His eyes lit up looking at the different options. "I wouldn't suggest the lip stain; it'd be really difficult to remove." he whispered.

"That would be a problem." I said. "They have flavored ones; it says it's cherry. Isn't that strange?" I pointed to the silver metal tube.

"You think so many things are strange. I think it'd be nice to try."

"Is that the one you want?" I asked, almost chuckling. He nodded. I asked the lady to bring that out for us. She handed it to me like it was a gem. Oliver paid for it at a very beautiful cash register with many metal buttons. We also saw mascara that came in many different types as well, and rouges that were creams and powders and of many different colors: pinks, reds, and browns. We ended up with some rouge. Oliver happily carried the bag.

I sent word to my family to come over for dinner on Thursday. I made a nice vegetable roast with good seasoning, wheat buns, and a cake to finish off with. I worked for days to make everything perfect, but I wanted my family to bring a sense of normalcy to my life, even if it was only for dinner. Oliver all the while was cleaning the house to avoid any type of questionable item. Even if my family went through every room of the house there would be no sight of cosmetics, alcohol, or dresses that I couldn't fit into, or wigs. Nothing. We were going to be an average, boring, perfectly Christian married couple, for now, and no one would be the wiser, and I could try to get back to being... happy.

Although I must admit that I didn't know what happiness truly was. I felt contentedness, brief periods of elation, but to reach actual happiness... I wasn't there yet, and truthfully, I didn't need to be there yet. I was very comfortable with myself, which was new enough for me, I knew what made me smile, and that was usually connected with nature. I could see admire from afar to focus on all the things that were far freer than I.

Mother came with Father first, and she looked around the house. She analyzed the space like a policeman looking for contraband. "Very nice, and clean. I'm surprised." Mama smiled a bit, she hardly ever smiled. She opened all the cupboards. "This porcelain and china, very classy Oliver." Oliver nodded, resting against the cupboard which we scrubbed and shined just hours before. I didn't want to hear anything negative coming from Mama's mouth tonight. I didn't have room for that. She walked into the living room and looked at the radio. "This is a new model, how did you afford all of these things, Oliver?"

"I was promoted at the bank and before the wedding I took up a lot of extra work to save money." Oliver said. Father stood next to him, trying to be more of a comforting force against my mother than an intimidating one. She stood next to the rocking chair.

"Are you thinking about children yet?" Mama asked.

I swallowed down a large lump that had formed in my throat and we looked at each other. "We haven't decided to have children yet."

"Well why not? You are in a stable position right now, wonderful home, and money to afford it." She turned to us and I nodded.

"I suppose we could consider the possibility." I added. I already brought it up to Oliver; he was the one who needed to be convinced.

"Very nice. I need a real grandchild. I may as well say that before your brother shows." She chuckled, her positive mood was rather alarming but it was better than how she could be acting. "May I see the rest of the house?"

"Of course, of course." I said, "Washroom and bedroom are just down the hall."

Father smiled and said, "Looks like you've put her in a good mood. This might last for days! She'll have such fun telling all her friends how wonderful a home you have." He patted Oliver's back with some force.

"Thank you Mr. Patterson." Oliver said. I checked the vegetables and it smelled heavenly. I had been hungry all day smelling this cook. The door opened and Clarence and Minnie walked in with Joy.

"Hello!" Minnie called. "I brought flowers!"

"Wonderful!" I said, greeting her. The house just lit up with the family being here. Everything was perfect.

Joy clung to the door, petting one of our white barn cats. She sat down as the cat curled in her lap purring loudly enough I could hear the rumble in the kitchen. When Clarence and Minnie sat down at the kitchen table, joined by mother I realized it was one of those moments above contentedness where we were all sitting around a table, smiling, laughing, talking. It didn't seem that bad to one day have a table full of children as well, babbling along, hands sticky and faces bright. I could only imagine how grateful to God I would be for that opportunity.

That night I sat in bed, combing my hair out, a process that took up a great deal of my morning and night routine. "Will you change your mind about having a child?" I asked.

He took a deep breath and turned to me. "I don't know. Let me have some time to think about it, alright?" I sighed loudly. "Is your mind already made up?"

"Possibly." I responded with a smile. He kissed my cheek and closed his eyes briefly. "What are you afraid of?"

"I don't want them to be like me." he said, his voice just above a sigh.

"What do you mean?" I asked, sitting up, pulling the sheet with me, balling it in my hands.

He chuckled and said, "I'm an invert. That's what they call people like me, perverts, unnatural people..." I sighed heavily and he said, "You know that too. I know you're angry with me about it. I can't change it.'

"I didn't say you could." I responded. "But I don't think that's hereditary."

"We don't know that." he said.

"I don't think you should be scared." I said, looking to my hands.

"You've been avoiding me since Albert." he said quietly. I fell silent and bit my lip. "We said there wasn't going to be a continuing relationship."

"Because he doesn't want to get fired from his professorship..." I said. "That doesn't mean you don't want to be with him!"

"That's not what I said." he said, crossing his arms.

"What did you mean?"

"I want to be with you, Virginia. That's why I married you."

"You could have done that so your uncle wouldn't question you about anything. How would I know? I didn't know hardly anything about you when I married you apparently."

"Virginia, I dedicated my life to helping you build yours." he said, moving so he sat cross legged in front of me, making eye contact in the dim light of early night. "Everything I do is for you."

Life went on as it was supposed to, day by day, night by night, getting covered in flour and washing off, feeding the chickens, gathering the eggs, resting in a homemade hammock amongst the trees. I wanted to take in as much of the summer as I possibly could while it lasted. Winter was my least favorite part of the year, and of living in general. I didn't like feeling trapped amongst the snow and the ice, nor the feeling of cold absolutely pervading my body. So, for the moment, I'd just bask in the sun, amongst the wind and the sweet air.

While Oliver and I were lounging around in the hammock I said, "You want to learn to swim, well then, you're going to learn to swim!" I chuckled and rolled over on him, kissing his cheek. He sighed and shook his head. I yanked on his arm and I flopped out of the hammock. "Come on, Oliver!" I said with a laugh. "You can do it, it's not that scary. I promise." He stood up off the hammock and onto the chicken dotted lawn. They scurried when we approached them and we quietly followed the road down to the pond. I held his hand in mine and skipped along a bit. Oliver smiled and shook his head. "You really don't know what real fun is."

"What does that mean?" I asked, looking him in the eye, stopping.

The smile on his face remained steady. "Jumping into a filthy farm pond isn't fun."

"You're whiny." I responded. I kissed his arm and continued to pull him along the road. He was tarrying on purpose. When we stepped up to the small pond, heavily surrounded by a thick line of trees, I stepped up to the muddy shore and looked at him, a smile pasted on my face. The birds flew above us in the hot sky.

"I'm supposed to get in that?" he chuckled, pointing.

"Uh huh." I said, pulling off my boots and stockings.

"Ginny, what are you doing?" he asked with a heavy sigh.

"I'm going in and so are you. Come on."

He whispered close to me, "Without your clothes?"

"I don't have a bathing suit." I reached up to the zipper on the back of my dress and stepped out, crossing my arms. "Well?" The heat decreased significantly without all the weight of the fabric on my body.

"Uh… we're outside, Ginny." Oliver whispered.

"Oliver. I let you take me to a hotel while you were wearing a dress and a wig, on numerous occasions. This is nothing in comparison. Nothing."

He sighed and started to unbutton his shirt, slipping out of his trousers. "I feel foolish." he said quietly. I stepped into the cold mud before stepping into the significantly warmer water. A majority of the water's surface was in direct contact with sunlight, only some of it was in the shade of the tall trees. I pulled him into the water until we were up to our waists. We both sucked in air from the shock.

"All these years we spent time here and you haven't gotten in the water… there's a drop off up here." I pointed. "All you need to do is remember to breathe, kick your legs, and move your arms like this." I demonstrated and kicked off into the water. He looked incredibly uncomfortable. I landed on my tip toes and bounced around in the water. "Come on, Oliver!"

"Uh…" he muttered, and he started splashing around like a monkey once he stepped off from the drop off.

"Do it just like I showed you!" I called to him. "Oliver, like this!" He lunged back into shallower water. I showed him again, coming next to him, standing up. He tried and appeared to have his head together this time and we moved deeper into the murky water. "There you go, you're doing well!" I said, trying to stay well above the water, but I was significantly shorter than Oliver and when he could still touch the floor, I couldn't.

"I swam!" he said with a smile on his face. "Huh…" He took in a deep breath and pulled his fingers through his loose wet hair.

"Keep going, keep going." I said, pulling on his arm even deeper into the water where he couldn't touch the ground. I kept on swimming through the cold green water to the other side of the small pond. It wasn't a clean piece of water, I could feel the seaweed and what climbing up around my feet. "Oliver!" I waved to him, trying to catch my breath. I was so close to the other side, with a few more good kicks I found myself touching the ground again.

"What are you doing, Virginia?" he screeched.

"It's not that scary, you can do it!" I called over, standing up, the water around my neck now.

"I just learned to do one stroke and you think I could go the entire way? What madness has gotten into you?"

"It's fun!" I called to him. "Just feel how the water holds you up! Supports you!"

He shook his head and dunked himself under the water first before attempting to swim in my direction, staying in the shallowest part. I swam toward him and once we reached each other I hugged him tightly, wrapping my legs around him and rested my head in the crook of his neck. "I love you." I said. He chuckled a bit and kissed my ear. "Still not liking the water?" I asked.

"I didn't say I don't like the water." he said with a laugh. I placed my lips on his and warmly pressed my body to his. "This isn't proper, Ginny," he whispered.

"Since when have you ever cared about being proper?" I asked, pulling my hair behind my head. "Alright, well, let's get back home and on dry land."

Albert's words, though, continued to haunt me. I did see peace around me in the late summer. If the world was truly ill and dying, it wouldn't look as it did. In a few months though, it'd look as dead as a skeleton, but would soon rejuvenate itself as it always did. It didn't seem, to me, that the world was following much of a linear pattern at all, or that it was all going towards an inevitable end like I had been taught. The world died every year, but eventually came back to life every spring. Albert, in his own way could be right, but ignoring everything I'd been taught my entire life seemed just as wrong as not looking for the truth. What truth was there for me to find anyways? I wasn't an inquisitive person by nature. I always felt very comfortable with just being comfortable, but there was a sense of restlessness now, all due to Oliver's incessant want for change. The restlessness was due to the fact that I didn't know anything. Father used to joke that a man's true wisdom only came from knowing that he knew nothing. And I didn't know how the world worked, how it would continue on, what would happen after death, nor what would happen in my own future.

That was always the mysterious thing about life. No one rarely is able to see their past clearly, nor understand their present acutely, nor can they even guess the future, no matter how many well-made plans existed. God was interesting that way. Our plans are our plans, not God's. God has His own ideas and goals, no matter how seemingly awful, or reckless, or glorious. And in most cases, humans are blind to everything in the world. I surely was. My world was small, and curious, but otherwise stable and monotonous. I didn't exist in a war-torn region where it would truly feel like the world was coming to an end. I didn't even get to experience the fear of a global flu epidemic. We were untouched. Perry would say it was because we were sheltered by God's power, but it only felt like we were sheltered from reality itself, and although as grateful as I was for that, it made me feel less than human. I didn't see as much, and didn't feel as much.

For me, God was both distant and immediate. He as a being felt far, far away, out of my grasp of knowledge or under-standing, yet not towering above me looking down as Reverend Perry would like to think. I saw God in everything: the trees, the grass, the bugs, the wind, animals, rain, storms, everything, between the demure and the powerful. Nature was God at his most honest, without the tainting of mankind, because I did believe that the awful nature of mankind did have a tainting effect on God. For some time, it made God a hateful, spiteful being, and I don't know if it really changed, but God was never angry with Nature; God was in harmony with it. We were des-perately trying to stand out from Nature, to conquer it, destroy it in some ways, or even ignore its existence. We worked against God. That much I did 'know'. In any case, I was most likely wrong about God, God was still an all knowing being that I was sure didn't look like a man, and thus what did I know?

I was told most of my life by Amos Perry that what Oliver was doing, dressing like a woman and having relationships with men was wrong, but I felt nothing unnatural about it; the only unnatural thing I was feeling was something resembling jealousy that he may be interested in someone other than me. He acted so free when he was out wearing that dress or when he was home. He had this look in his eyes of joy just by being himself. He lived in a way I didn't comprehend how to access. I didn't know what the word freedom meant, nor how to achieve it. Oliver was trying to teach me. The only thing I chose in my life was him, and I was still learning from that choice what choices could do. You could end up with a crossing dressing homosexual with an affinity for pearls and cosmetics, and yet I loved him dearly.

At the beginning of fall, when the wind became bitter and crisp, I asked Minnie if I could have a few of her late sister's dresses to make her a memory quilt. I thought if I could put something together to make her and Joy happy, I would be able to do something worthwhile during the colder months. Already, I was becoming unnerved by the colder weather, even if it had only been around for a few days.

Minnie was very excited about it, and her entire face lit up. The following day, she very happily brought over a heavy wooden box stuffed full of the crisp, musty dresses that hadn't been touched since the woman's death. I arranged for Clara to come to the house to tailor a few dresses for Oliver. It was the best I could do to give something back to my husband, to make changes within the house for him. At the same time, though, it felt almost sacrilegious to have Minnie's late sister's dresses being fitted for a man. I didn't know what the woman's beliefs were, if she would be rolling in her grave…

Clara drove to the house in their gorgeous automobile. She wore a black hat which kept close to her equally black hair. She carried herself with all the confidence in the world.

Her sewing kit was in a red silk covered box with oriental embroidery. She placed it to the side as she entered the house and embraced both of us. Quickly I got Oliver to stand atop a wooden box while I hung all the dresses on the couch. Clara rummaged through her sewing kit, eventually pulling out well-cared for shears in a leather bag. All of the dresses I had were too wide for Oliver's body since he was just a twig.

I handed Oliver a light pink dress with a bit of lace around the chest and he pulled it over his body. Immediately Clara pinned up the excess cloth that would eventually be used in the memory quilt. "This woman was a giant." Clara muttered, stretching out the quilt.

"Apparently. This dress feels very heavy." Oliver said, lifting up the cloth from around his feet. "But it is very nice, nonetheless. Thank you for getting this for me, Ginny."

"Of course." I said, sitting in the rocking chair.

"We should find a place to take you in this," Clara said, standing up and adjusting the collar. "You should wear that nice pinkish lipstick with this one so you don't look so flushed."

"What's wrong with the hotel?" I asked.

"Doesn't going to the same place repeatedly get quite boring?" Clara asked, patting Oliver's cheek.

"I suppose…" I muttered, but some heat entered into my chest. The hotel was safe. I wasn't sure about the rest of the world.

"See if we could go into the city, possibly to an opera, or a play," Clara said. "That would be a wonderful experience, George always asks if we can find an occasion to go. He's a man of the arts."

"I wouldn't say I am." Oliver said, taking in a deep breath. The wind outside was so high that the house shook just slightly. "I'm a chicken farmer."

"A man of the arts?" I asked. "I wouldn't say you are either. A banker sounds a bit better if you were trying to choose a title."

"I think in about a month there's a version of Macbeth coming out soon. I've always wanted to see it…"

There was a sudden knock at the door and we all froze. Oliver's face was covered in absolute fear and all color drained from his skin. I didn't even mange to stand up fast enough to do anything about it when Amos Perry came charging through the door. I realized I forgot to send him his order of communion bread. He froze in the same way we did when he faced Oliver who was trying to hide his face. Absolute disgust was painted all about our preacher. "What is the meaning of this, Oliver?" he managed to bellow.

Oliver looked like he was trying to speak but nothing came out of his mouth. Reverend Perry's face was beet red and his neck was strained. He shook his head and said, "You are an abomination! You are supposed to be a responsible man! A husband! The rock of your household and here you are in women's dress, looking like a pathetic mess! Have you never listened to all the knowledge I have given to you? The wicked shall be cut off! They shall not inherit the land of the Lord! You should fear what can destroy your soul! You must repent! Turn back to God or you will perish!" Reverend Perry was genuinely scared by what he saw. I knew he loved his nephew, it was evident in his anger. If he didn't care, he wouldn't be screaming in that young man's face.

"My soul is my own. James chapter four verse twelve: there is only one lawgiver and judge, he who is able to save and to destroy, but who are you to judge your neighbor?"

Amos fell quiet and stared ahead, then walked very quickly out the door, slamming it behind him. "What was that?" Clara asked.

"My uncle. Maybe we should be finished now…" Oliver said, deflated, his voice cracking a bit. I was amazed he said anything at all to his uncle, but even more so that it was memorized scripture.

"Oh dear," I walked up to him. "You know what he's saying cannot be the truth."

"He thinks I'm the wicked or evil even… He must hate me…" Oliver stepped down from the wooden box and Clara helped him get out of the dress. There were tears welling up in the poor man's eyes.

"No, no, he's just scared. He doesn't understand, that's why he's scared." I put my hands on his face and tried to make eye contact. "I believe in your judgement, Oliver. What is natural to you cannot possibly be wicked."

"That man knows every line of scripture…"

"That doesn't mean he's interpreted it correctly, dear." I breathed, realizing that Albert could actually be right, and that was still potentially terrifying.

"You don't understand," he breathed, pulling his shirt on. "If he tells anyone, this isn't just about me anymore, dear, it's about you too."

Clara asked, "Should I leave for now? So you two may speak?"

"Thank you, Clara," Oliver said. "I appreciate that you came."

"Please let me know if you would like me to continue on, and let me know if you need anything, anything at all." Clara said, stepping outside, giving us a small wave. Soon the engine of her automobile started, and it puttered away.

Oliver collapsed on the couch and closed his eyes. "Why did he even come?" he asked.

"Please, calm down. We will be alright." I pressed. "There is nothing to worry about." I didn't want to admit that I didn't complete his order. This was my fault. It was my mistake.

"You are insane." He laughed angrily, shaking his head. He closed his eyes and lay down on the couch across all the dresses. The cat jumped in through the window and jumped onto his stomach and lay down. He smiled and pet the white cat's ears. I knelt next to him and tried to look as calm as possible. "I'm… I'm just going to go to bed. I need some sleep." He stood up and took the cat with him without hardly acknowledging my presence.

Chapter Ten

We stood in front of the mirror. I placed my hat on my head and pinned it in place. Oliver adjusted his tie. We decided we were going to go on like normal, and Saturday church was part of that normal routine. He had been very quiet for the past few days since Amos barged into our house. Oliver's heart was beating quickly. I could feel it. "We'll be alright," I assured him again, wrapping my arm around his. It was strange being near him when he was like this. He didn't feel like he was any of the Olivers I married. He was an unexpectedly beaten puppy.

Oliver drove, and instead of smiling, talking, laughing, slouching, he was silent and straight as an arrow. The crisp air whipped through the sky. About now the trees were really turning, but being surrounded by pines, there were only a few trees turning into the colors of fire. A few fields became nothing more than cattle feed after the crops were pulled up and picked.

When we arrived, and entered the church, it fell silent. Usually there was always an overarching hum of talking and whispering, but at the moment I could hear the birds chirping outside, even moving from branch to branch and the wind in the drying leaves. There were eyes all over us, looking but avoiding us all at the same time. Clarence stepped up to me discreetly and put a hand on my shoulder. "It'd be best if Oliver wasn't here." he whispered.

"Why?" I asked.

"Amos announced that he was not welcome here any longer."

"We are staying." I stated. I seized Oliver's hand and took a seat in the back pew, away from my parents, or my brother, or anyone else for that matter. Clarence stood for a moment near the door of the sanctuary before biting his lip and joining my parents once again. Minnie turned to look at me with pleading eyes, with Joy in her lap. Oliver's eyes were shaking and he was swallowing incessantly. "Calm down, Oliver." I said. "They can probably smell your fear."

"They probably can." he responded. "I'm sweating like a pig."

"You're alright, I'm here, I'm here..." I didn't know if that made it alright.

Amos stood at the head of the congregation, his hands together. He paced for a moment, waiting for the sanctuary to be completely silent. "We cannot forget who we are. We cannot forget what we are." Amos said quietly. "But it seems that human nature is locked in that original sin. We cannot seem to help ourselves but to forget, to lose our way, to get lost, walking on the path of unrighteousness and death rather than life! We do not have the liberty to be so loose. Law is law, not a suggestion. There are consequences to break the law. It is dangerous, to us, to the end, to God, to the remnant church that has been ordained to forget the law. In the book of Corinthians, it says: or do you not know that the unrighteous will not inherit the kingdom of God? Do not be deceived, neither the sexually immoral, nor idolaters, nor adulterers, nor men who practice homosexuality, nor thieves, nor the greedy, nor drunkards, nor revilers, nor swindlers will inherit the kingdom of God. Matthew says no one can serve two masters, for either he will hate the one and love the other, or he will be devoted to the one, and despise the other. You cannot serve both God, and anything else. You must be devoted to God alone. Walk by the spirit and you will not gratify the desires of the flesh! And Jesus said to his disciples, 'you shall love the Lord your God with all your heart and all your soul and with all your mind, this is the great and first commandment." Amos didn't even start with a hymn, he just spoke in the silence, his voice going through the sanctuary, bouncing off the wooden walls.

Oliver shook his head, shaking and he whispered, "The second is like it. You shall love your neighbor as yourself." He looked to me with pleading eyes. "I can't stay, Virginia." He stood up and left the sanctuary as quietly as he could. The sanctuary fell silent again and eyes turned back to me. There was so much tension and energy in the air that I stood up and followed right after him, if not just to get away from those eyes. Oliver was standing in the sun, looking up at the sky like he was going to cry out to God. He remained silent. I stepped up to him and placed my hand on his arm.

"What was that?" I asked.

"That was about me! He was speaking directly to me!" he cried. "I have to go back home. I can't stay here... I can't..."

He went to the cart and got in. I quietly followed. My heart was wrenched at the moment with shame and confusion, if not some pity as well. It was silent the entire way back. My mind floated off into the sky. When we arrived home, Oliver very quickly let the horse out in the pasture and put the cart inside the barn. I stood in front of the massive ash tree standing beside the house. "Oliver..." I muttered. "Are you alright?"

He turned to me and stared straight ahead. There was only pain on his face. I stepped up to him. "Oliver..." I put my hand on his cheek. He was burning up.

"They know, they all know..." He shook his head and turned away, shaking, pacing.

"It's alright, Oliver. We... we just need to stop then."

"Stop what?" he cried.

"Stop with the dresses and the makeup and the drinking... then it'll all be better. They won't do anything."

"It doesn't work like that! It didn't work when my father found me with my mother's pearls and her shoes and he threw me against a wall and beat me! Or when he told my uncles and they all took a switch to my back next to the creek so my mother couldn't hear! It didn't work when they threatened to hang me from a tree... It doesn't get rid of the thoughts!" There were tears welling up in his eyes.

"We should go inside..." I breathed, trying to stay calm.

"Are you even listening to me?"

"Of course I am Oliver," I took his hand and we went inside. I sat down at the old rocking chair, trying to keep myself together. There were too many nerves in my stomach. "I need you to answer me, honestly..." He sat down as well, across from me. "Do you love me?"

He moved towards me and took my hands, resting his head on my legs. "Ginny, I've wanted to marry you since I first met you, even when we were four years old, I dreamed of being your husband."

"Then why do you do this? Dress like that?"

"Because it's... it's like a release... it's comfortable that way... I can breathe...I don't know how to explain it to you past that."

"I don't understand." I said.

"Neither do I!" he cried. "I can't help it… I thought I could keep it away from them, they'd never know and then they'd think I was just… just normal."

"I don't know why we can't become normal." I whispered.

"They couldn't beat it out of me, Ginny… they couldn't scream it out of me. I couldn't scream it out of me."

"Then I guess that's the way things are."

"And what does that mean for us?" he asked.

"I don't know… I don't know…"

I didn't like silence at all but there was quite was some concern that someone would come up the road, and for whatever reason, I felt Oliver's fear. I went back outside, to keep watch on the road to put Oliver at ease, at least partially. As I stood underneath of the tree, pacing, I decided that the Sabbath was already ruined, what was being productive? Sitting inside was going to be far more uncomfortable than working with the chickens.

The chicken coop for the egg laying hens was surrounded by some nice wire my father ordered to keep the hens away from the others so there wouldn't be any more chicks then necessary. I went inside and collected the eggs in a basket and set it aside. The chickens scurried about; some being brave enough to walk up to me. Most of them were tame enough to pet if I sat down long enough. I went inside the coop and started to replace all the hay and gave them new water.

The other grouping were the male chicks who were culled every once in a while depending on what father needed for the store. Some non-Adventist individuals bought the meat. There was a sizeable flock that roamed pretty freely around here, although I needed to bring them inside their own coop regularly to get them away from the fox and hawk population that loved to eat them.

Once I finished caring for the chickens, I sat down in the pen and waited for the hens to come up to me. Some of them would lie down next to me. There was an almost meditative quality about just petting the animals. They were so simple; their minds were nothing more than what was needed for survival. They held emotions that were no more than fear, contentedness, comfort even. At the moment, it was comfort. It was clear when their hearts slowed, their eyelids closed, their heads drooped. My mother used to do the same then she was going to break their necks for the store. Chickens would fall for it every time. None of these chickens were in any danger of me breaking their necks anytime soon. That was my father's job, I was, after all this time, still too queasy to do it.

Oliver stepped out and the chickens awoke and went back to their normal routine of milling about, occasionally breaking into periods of sprinting. He stood on the other side of the fence. "Ginny... I need to leave." he said quietly.

"Leave?" I asked, trying to stand up. One of my feet had fallen asleep and was tingling horribly.

"I... it's not safe. I've had a friend who was... he was beaten to death for wearing a dress." he breathed, looking away. He avoided eye contact. He hardly ever avoided eye contact.

"And you think that will happen to you?" I walked out of the coop and took his hand. "You think those people would do something so violent?"

"I don't feel safe, Ginny..." he quietly responded. "Maybe I just need to have a break from everyone for a while... maybe they'll forget."

"And where are you going to go?" I asked, anger starting to gather in my throat.

"Possibly I could go see Albert for some time, try to clear my head..."

"Albert? Albert? Truly? No, no, no, you are not leaving me to go to him. That's not acceptable." I cried. "You are my husband. I need my husband here."

"Ginny, I'm leaving just for a little while… I'm coming back. I promise. I don't want to wait too long and risk it… it's happened before. People like me are killed…" he breathed.

"I don't understand…" I muttered, moving away from him. "I don't know why you even wanted to marry me if you were just going to run off back to your old lover, and a man for God's sake! That isn't fair to me, at all. Don't you even think about that?"

"I… I…" he stopped and took in a deep breath and shook his head. "I told you what I am doing. Virginia. That's it. It's for both of our safety."

"And when is this happening?"

"Tomorrow morning." he responded. "The sooner I'm gone, the safer we both are."

"You are insane. You must be. You have to be…" I was absolutely shaking, but I tried to calm myself down.

"I need you to support me, Ginny. I have no one else to do so."

Chapter Eleven

I was taught as a girl to ignore emotions. Anything, everything. Happiness, sadness, anger especially, elation, grief, so I had never been taught how to deal with them if they were too powerful to ignore. I sat on the porch of the house on the swinging chair with the cat beside me. Oliver was gone. He was on the road to Albert's elaborate house. Even within a few moments, I felt utterly alone. It was very early in the morning, I sipped at my tea, focusing on how warm it was, following it down into my stomach, through my throat. The cat was purring underneath my hand, pressing her head into mine.

I wished I could ignore what was happening in my mind. It hurt, and it would continue to hurt. I walked around the house, barefooted. I had to go to work today, but I didn't want anyone to see my face, and that included my father, my brother, anyone at all. I took the long walk to the general store with the basket of eggs on my arm. The wind rushed past me, blasting my face with the crisp air. It smelled of freshly cut hay and the thick scented pine of the forest in the distance. I always wanted to know what was in there. Mama said that ladies aren't supposed to get dirty. I didn't particularly care what she said at the moment. Anger was a very interesting emotion. I felt like I didn't like anyone, including myself.

When I got to the general store, Clarence looked at me nervously. "Are you two alright?" he asked. "After Saturday?"

"Oliver left." I responded. "He says he doesn't feel safe here anymore."

"He's probably right. People don't treat men like him real good around here."

He touched my shoulder, attempting to comfort me. I nodded, without saying anything else, and went into my room and got to work. I did everything in my power to close my mind to any incoming thoughts, but it was incredibly difficult. There were far too many things to decipher, too many answers that I didn't have, but wanted.

Over the next week, nothing got better. The general store was deserted. No one came to us. They'd rather go to town to get their things rather to my father. "Am I some kind of disease?" I asked Father when he walked in.

He looked at me, confused for a moment. His face was gaunt and sad. "Ginny, I think it'd be better if you worked from home." he said.

"What is happening here?" I asked, crying.

"Virginia…" he sighed. "I'll see you later. You'll still get work…"

"Father… I don't know what's happening," I said.

"Neither do I." he responded. He hugged my tightly, pressing his furry cheek against mine. The embrace felt forced, uncomfortable. When he let go, he looked me in the eye. I stepped back and sat on the stool in my workroom, feeling the wind rush in from outside, and hit me. I closed my eyes for a moment; shame and anger rushed through my veins, pulsing from my heart. I was a disease. This simple event managed to ruin everything I ever worked for. Any sense of contentedness I had was gone. I was so shocked I couldn't move. I just stared ahead at the wooden displays in the center of the store. This place was built with my work, and I had to leave.

As soon as I walked through the front door of the house I sat at the kitchen table, I sent some correspondence to Clara and George so I would have some type of communication, but otherwise, I was alone in the house. The house seemed so large and empty. I kept cleaning and kept organizing. I wanted everything to be perfect. It was the only way I'd be able to cope. I put the dresses away back in Oliver's wooden box along with the wig. I paced a lot. Worked on some sewing, trying to work on Minnie's memory quilt, but never found that to be enjoyable in the least. Nothing solved the restlessness.

Three days after being told by my father I couldn't work from the general store, while it was still warm, I walked toward the edge of the forest. I was curious and had nothing else to do with my time or energy. The forest seemed so far into the distance, but within a few long moments of walking, I was almost there. The forest grew in size as I got closer, the trees grew taller, and the light around it was different than the light in or out of a house. It wasn't so blue, it was far more golden, bright, lively. I stepped in, being consumed, surrounded by the forest. High above me the trees reached, almost blocking out the sky. They intertwined with one another, letting the light through only in visible beams that danced upon the bright green leaves and the decaying foliage on the ground. The ground itself was alive. There was ivy, thorny branches growing in a carpet and many lacy ferns. I stepped carefully through, holding up my skirt as I felt the cold ground crunch beneath me. It smelled of death and life, combined.

There was nothing more peaceful than this moment, despite my being alone. It felt as if I was truly a soul. That I was an individual plunged into a living land that I knew very little about, surrounded by the nature of God, and everything that he protected graciously. This was the handiwork of God. This was art as it was meant to be.

There were little flowers growing on the ground, small yellow flowers that were in bunches. There were individual purple flowers that were the size of my thumb near the trunks of some of the tallest trees. They were exquisite little creatures; the individual petals were waxy and bright. As I continued through the forest, making a straight line as not to get lost I winded up in a clearing where the grass was piled and smooth and soft. I lay down amongst it and stared up at the fluffy, pastel sky, surrounded still by tall thin trees with bleached bark. I could stay here for some time, I thought, and I did. There was no need to think, do, or answer to anything for some time, just to exist, to breathe, to smell what was around me. It was truly being alive.

I suddenly felt like I had been hindered for so long in my life from actually being a living being. The world was not supposed to be made of stone, or dead wood. It felt as if everything I saw was a lie. Those who I knew, who thought they had God's answers, what did they truly know? I'd never seen God before, but I did now. Everywhere. The gold dancing around me was God. God was in this forest. He wasn't in those buildings. He wasn't in their relics or their gold, or those crosses. Why would he be? This was the place any person should wish to be.

Yet peace was only so long lived. Bugs lived here too and I didn't like them crawling on me. They were getting far more comfortable with my being here a great deal faster than the chickens even. I stood up and looked around, and as familiar as I was getting with this forest in one day, I still forgot which direction I came from. So I made sure that I recognized the flowers as I walked back.

Responsibility was more important in my mind than anything else, and although I hated leaving the forest, I trudged back, feeling both rejuvenated, and yet drained of all energy. I fed the chickens and went inside, getting something to eat, although lately I'd been eating little more than bread, butter, and eggs. There was no need to make anything extravagant if I wasn't going to taste it.

Clara and George received my letters came to visit. I sat on the rocking chair outside on the porch with a quilt on my lap. They stepped up and sat down on the white porch swing. Their presence was so strange. People. I hadn't seen people in a long time except Clarence coming by to pick up bread and eggs to sell. It was a hug, a hello, and nothing else, a face that betrayed nothing more than shame. Clara and George had seen Oliver in a dress and they didn't give the expression of shame. Now I got pity though. What was it I looked like?

"How are you doing?" Clara asked softly, reaching out to touch my knee.

"I just didn't think he'd just up and leave." I responded, shaking my head.

"It's very much unlike him." George said. "I wish we had good news for you."

"I'm glad you came." I said. "It's been very lonely here."

"I'd imagine. You're out in the middle of nowhere. Are you still working?" Clara asked.

I nodded. "Yes, and I'm being paid for my work, but my Father thought that my presence at the store was making it so the people of our church didn't want to come there… no one came in the store after the pastor came in and saw Oliver."

"You think he told everyone?" George asked.

"I know he did." I said with a heavy sigh. "Clarence told me."

"I think it would be nice for you to go on an automobile ride." Clara said suddenly. "You need to get away from this place. You've been here too long, alone."

"Do you ever miss horses?" I asked.

Clara shook her head. "Horses have opinions and quirks, cars don't."

"That's what you say," George huffed. "That car over there takes just as much care as a horse. It's just as expensive too. The only way it's helpful is it's fast, and it feels powerful."

"Men and power, I don't understand. If you can't go about killing each other in pointless wars, you go on building and driving automobiles so you can feel like... well, I shouldn't go there." She smirked and shook her head a little bit.

"She's been reading up on her insults." George says. "All those English novels and all."

"Are you not working then?" I asked.

"I do the inventory and reservations at the hotel." George said.

"I don't have the ability to stare at such dullness for that long of a period of time." Clara added with a flick of her hand.

"Are you saying I have nothing better to do?" George asked, looking partially spooked.

"I'm saying that your mind can take it when I can't." she said and crossed her arms. "He gets so confused by things. Can't you see?" I smiled a bit.

"She just likes to be rude." George said. "Recently, we've been stepping away a little from the hotel, working just on the management rather than going to the parties so much. Maybe it's stressing her out."

"No, no, no, I've been getting these absolutely wretched headaches." Clara exclaimed, pointing her finger at George who smiled slyly.

"Have you gotten any remedies for them?" I asked.

"She doesn't trust drugs." George quickly replied. "Nor doctors really."

"The lights, and the sound, and the alcohol, don't particularly help, so sitting in a nice quiet room with a book, they almost go away."

"Hence her catching up on a library of reading," George mumbled. "Would you be interested if we brought you a few books?"

"I don't read very well; I only took up through fourth grade." I said.

"We should at least get you some groceries. You don't look like you've eaten hardly anything for a while." George said. "How about we come back in a few days with food?"

I nodded. "I apologize that all of this is happening, and bringing you into it."

Clara's face contorted. "No, no, no, I'm glad you contacted us. There's nothing more we want to do than help you out, Virginia. Alright?"

"May I ask why?" My voice cracked a bit.

The two looked at each other for a moment, light in their eyes. It was comforting. "Because you're a friend of ours. George and I have always made it a point to help out friends, no matter what."

"I can't help you though." I responded quietly.

"You don't need to. There's nothing we need help with at the moment." George responded. "Just relax, sweetie, and make sure you get enough food and rest. We'll be back in a few days." They stood up from the porch swing and went to their fancy automobile. They waved to me and I smiled a little as well.

I felt a little lighter than before. A little stranger too. I questioned how long I could exist like this, breathing, alive, but feeling so far from it. And all because I was alienated from everything I ever knew. My family thought I was contagious, a thing flowing with sin, and if sin was a crawling feeling right under the skin, then sure, I was filled with it. If it meant I felt alone, then yes. It was hellish. The feelings weren't logical in the least, but they were just there, and I didn't know how to get rid of them.

George came by two days later with a wooden box filled with food. He hardly knocked on the door and walked in before I could reach the living room. "Good morning, Virginia!" he called, walking quickly over to the kitchen table, placing down the box. He went up to the cupboard, clearly knowing where things belonged. He looked through the pantry and said, "This is pathetically empty. Bread? That's all?" I nodded. "Virginia…" He leaned against the counter and shook his head. "All of this because of Oliver? Because he left?" I shook my head. "Then explain it to me, I'd like to understand."

"I… thank you for the food, truly." I said looking in the box. There were jars of preserves of fruits and vegetables and some meat. I didn't know how to cook meat.

George took in a deep breath and nodded, smiling just a bit. He turned and looked through the window out to the yard that was dotted by colorful chickens. He touched where his hair was tied behind his head and then placed his head upon it. "Well, Mrs. Crain, I hope this helps." He nodded to me. "Clara and I will see you in a few days. If you need to speak to either of us, will you?"

"I do not know if I can promise anything right now." I said. "Thank you, George."

I wasn't every very hungry, but for the sake of Clara and George I ate from the wooden box, distributing the preserves and other assorted foods where they belonged in the kitchen. The cat jumped in through the window and rubbed her head against my chin and walked freely over the counter. She looked a little heavier than usual. I placed my hands on her sides and felt a few little lumps. "Looks like you are going to be a Mama." I said, looking at her a bit closer. She continued to purr, and jumped down from the counter gracefully, her feet hardly making a thump as she landed. She trotted back to the bedroom and took a spot in the middle of the bed. I followed after her, feeling the unseasonably warm wind blow through the open windows. I sat down beside her and lay on the bed, staring at the ceiling, my ears ringing in the silence until it was filled by the very calm motorized purring of the cat.

In a matter of days, in a little box in the living room the mama cat had all her little babies. They were there when I woke up one morning, small little pink round bundles of fur of multiple colors. Their eyes were closed and their ears were little, and their legs were stumpy. They kept close to their mother who was fast asleep when I found her. There were seven little babies alive, and there was one who wasn't. I buried the little thing outside amongst the rose bushes.

When I came back inside I mixed some eggs together for the mama who very happily took to it, her teats all swollen and hanging low as she drank. She kept looking at me with something that was similar to suspicion. The babies cried with little snips when she was away. I went to a cupboard in the bedroom and brought out some colorful ribbons. With all the supplies that Clara brought to fix the dresses that were once intended for Oliver, there were many different types of ribbons left in my living room. I sat down beside the babies and gave them each their own color of ribbon before I went back to work on Minnie's memory quilt for her sister Sally.

Instead of it being baby sized as I once thought, now I had enough material to make it large enough to comfortably cover a bed. Although I wasn't skilled with quilting, it would consume some time. Although I rarely listened to the radio at home, I was quite willing to listen to it now. I needed to hear human voices, not just the sheep like bleating of the kittens and the distant clucking of chickens. While I was quilting in the living room with the curtains open with the last remaining light of the day, the mama cat stood up and ran outside briefly. I watched as she sat on the porch staring out around her. It was as if she was having all the complicated thoughts I was having recently. I understood but nonetheless it was a bit concerning that a cat could have thoughts, feelings, but with personality comes those emotions, and this cat had emotion.

I thought I should name her then. She was an off-white color with silver accents, so I called her Opal. She was majestic, even with her extra weight and the tiredness in her eyes. I always wondered why it was cats never betrayed pain. Never once did I hear her complain while giving birth to eight babies last night. Never did I ever see any cat act like something was hurting. Why was humanity so weak in comparison? It was written all over my face, it was written throughout my body, my bones, my blood, and for nothing. It was doing me no good to act this way.

I thought maybe I should just be like Opal. Stoic. To be like all those Romans who were of an age where weakness meant death and death was final. There were no second chances, and there were no easy outs. Possibly I could be successful then. Happy, potentially, or at least return to contentedness where I sat for a majority of my life. I could also be like Opal's kittens, new to the world, ignorant of all, blissfully resting amongst the warm cloth they were curled up in, happy to just lounge around and drink the milk they were supplied. They knew nothing, and they would grow to learn just a little bit more, how to survive, which was not taught through words but actions and instinct.

My life was formed by ignoring instinct. Human nature was supposedly a negative thing, leading only to sin and death. However, the longer I was away from Reverend Perry's teaching, I questioned why God would have formed such flawed creatures. Would instinct or tradition be the flawed part then? But I didn't hardly know scripture, nor did I know hardly any philosophy. I was as ignorant as those kittens when it came to God's truth. Was doing what felt right, right? At the moment, though, nothing *felt* right. Everything felt just a little wrong, strange.

While starting my work in the morning, I got the wood stove starting. The air was frosty, and there was no sense of heat in the house outside of the cocoon I made for myself in the bed. Wrapped in my warmest shawl, I got the oven started to heat up water to start the bread dough. Like clockwork I measured out exact amounts of flour, salt, and yeast. As soon as the sun raised above the horizon, sleet fell from the sky in heavy sheets. The sound was calming as it hit the roof steadily.

A puttering came up the to the house. Not expecting a visit from Clara or George, my heart beat quickly with adrenaline. There was never a day I was without fear. I wiped my hands off on my apron and nervously stepped up to the door. I couldn't see far due to the sleet and the wind. I locked the door and waited for the person to approach the porch. The heavy footsteps shook me to my core, but seeing through the glass, I saw it was Albert. He knocked on the door. I didn't want to answer, but opened the door. The cold rushed into the house. He held his hat to his chest and I asked, "What are you doing here?"

"I wanted to speak to you about Oliver,"

"No." I said, and slammed the door in his face. I turned back to the kitchen. With the water having become warm, I mixed it with the yeast and let it bubble slightly before stirring it into the flour mixture. My ears waited for the sound of the automobile engine to start. I didn't hear anything. I turned back and Albert was still on the porch, sitting on the swing, even in the cold and sleet. I didn't know if it was endearing or creepy. Regardless, I formed the first round of dough and placed it on a shelf above the stove so it would raise in the warmth. The rest of the house was still frigid, and probably would remain so throughout the day.

Albert's presence nagged at me, and I opened the door. "You're not leaving, are you?"

"I want to speak with you. May I come in?" he asked, removing his hat again. There was a sense he was being respectful.

"Why?" I hissed. "You mock my faith and then you steal my husband. What else do you want to take from me?"

"May I explain myself?" he asked. "Please."

"Come in," I said begrudgingly. I closed the door behind him. He hung his hat on the coat rack beside the door and stepped in. He looked out of place in my simple home. He looked like he belonged in his mansion. I moved back to the kitchen, and he followed me.

"I didn't ask for Oliver to come to my home, Virginia. He's just a… a house guest. He's afraid for his life." Albert said, sitting at the kitchen table. "I'm not going to turn him out until he's comfortable."

I shook my head and laughed angrily. "Does he not realize how uncomfortable I am? No one will speak to me. I haven't been able to leave this house hardly. I'm completely isolated."

"So is he." Albert said quietly.

"He did that to us." I pressed. "He and his dresses and his pearls…"

Albert took in a deep breath. "I realize what your congregation must think, but they're wrong about him."

"Here you go again." I breathed.

"I'm trying to give you comfort here." he said simply.

"By what? Telling me that what he's doing is alright?"

"Virginia…" He took in a deep breath. "Please just let me speak,"

"Tell me, have you… have you had sex with him since he's been at your house."

He nodded and said, "Yes."

I shook my head angrily and threw my apron onto the counter. "And you dare to walk through my door? Don't you realize how stupid I feel? Just months ago, I thought that I actually had a good home, and a future, and…"

"Virginia, I love Oliver," he said. "I honestly do, but I don't want to take him from you. I told you that I don't want to jeopardize my career. I don't want to raise any red flags… but,"

"But what?" I screamed, stepping closer to him. He held his breath for a moment. "I don't even know what I want anymore! I don't know if I'd be comfortable with having him in this house, but I'm not comfortable without him! I don't know what to do!"

He bit his lip and lowered his head. "Can I come by again on Sunday? I'd like you to go to mass with me."

"You're Catholic?" I screeched. "You of all people…"

"I just want to get you out of this house, into a community."

"I'm sure if they knew that you and my husband were homosexuals they'd ostracize you as well."

"I don't doubt that, but they aren't going to run into my house and see me in a dress. There's no risk. Please, just take me up on that offer. I'm trying to make peace here."

"Fine," I said with a heavy breath. I wanted to get out of this house too, I just wasn't courageous enough to do it yet.

Chapter Twelve

I appreciated the visits from Clara and George. They nagged at me to make sure I was eating sufficiently enough. If the food they brought me was not consumed, Clara had a tendency to complain until I did. George's eyes just glazed over when she started talking like that. It was laughable to see. I decided to be patient. As patient, as was necessary. So, I smiled, and if I smiled enough, the smiles became less fake. I could walk outside and look at the sky and twirl around and even dance to the radio, even if it was by myself. I could picture the dancefloor of the hotel in my mind, where all the people moved together. I could taste the thick, burning liquor, and remembered how horrible it made me feel and Oliver's wide, crinkling smile at my reaction. And at times, I actually felt light on my feet, with the sound of the growing kittens in the back ground, wandering around my feet. I was careful not to step on them, it was like they were dancing with me.

At night, I was surrounded by the kittens and Opal on my bed, feeling the purring and the warm balls of fur all around me. I was sleeping better than I ever had before. I just needed to learn. There was such thing as peace now, even after my mind had lost itself in the midst of being rejected by everything. I made the decision that God was truly real and could help me find this candle in the dark. I was grateful.

Albert drove by that Sunday, wearing a grey woolen suit. He looked different when he wasn't drenched in sleet. He stepped up to my door. I was in my normal church dress with my white woolen shawl. It'd been weeks since I left this land. Fear drenched me. All I wanted, was to get back to normalcy, and perhaps this could be a gateway to do so. Albert always took his hat off when he greeted me, and he smiled. "Good morning, Virginia." he said. I only nodded to him and stepped on the porch, looking back at Opal and her kittens sitting on my furniture. "Are you ready?" he asked. I nodded again. My mouth felt like it was glued shut.

He opened the door to the automobile for me and I sat inside. Even with the number of time's I'd been in an automobile, it was still strange to feel it come to life beneath me. He turned onto the main road. Everything looked nearly dead around me. It was that time of year. Albert looked at me a few times before saying, "You look well today." I nodded. "Are you going to speak?" He sounded amused rather than annoyed.

"I'm just tired." I said, folding my hands in my lap. Slowly I formed into what my mother would have expected of me. Just looking at Albert, I wanted to know what attracted Oliver to him. His face was chiseled, probably due to war, though. His skin was worn on the edges, but his hair was combed well beneath his flat hat. It was only in his face and his eyes that I could believe he was in the trenches in France. His clothing and demeanor suggested he lived a posh lifestyle, and lived comfortably. "Tell me about the war," I said.

"What do you want to know?" he asked.

"Why did you decide to go?"

"I love history. I wanted to be a part of it. I wasn't smart enough to realize I made a horrible decision."

"Looks like you came out alright," I responded.

He chuckled and took in a deep breath. He did that a lot when he was uncomfortable. "Physically, yes. I saw things I never should have seen." He turned right, passing through a thickly wooded area. It was still green with the pines, but fallen leaves littered the sides of the road. "So many other men died for nothing. It was a war of attrition; all that means is each side just tried to kill as many men as possible. It was a waste of life. There was no point to the war, we didn't get much out of it I don't think except for some money."

"Then why did the US get involved?"

"Trade routes…" he said. "I shouldn't have gotten involved myself. All I had to keep myself occupied was making those watches. I have yours here if you would like it back."

He touched a compartment beside his arm. I opened it and there it was, sitting on some tissue paper. "I made that for you." he said. "Oliver always spoke of you before I went over there, and in letters while I was there. I felt like I knew you before I met you. I apologize for everything that's happened since, although I feel like it's out of my control, what Oliver's doing."

I touched the wristwatch and removed it from the compartment and clasped it around my wrist. He smiled.

The Catholic church looked as isolated as I felt. He pulled into a space reserved mostly for carts and horses. Most of these people didn't have enough money for an automobile. We walked into the building together. There were no people meandering about outside like the last time I was here with Oliver. It was too cold out for that. When we entered, I analyzed the space around me for any familiar faces. Albert stepped forward and

I followed throughout the narthex. A few individuals greeted Albert, although most didn't recognize me from my previous visit. I introduced myself as Virginia Crain. Patrick jogged up to me and said, "I haven't seen you in quite some time! Either of you!" he said. He patted Albert's shoulder with some gusto. "You've only been here once since you came back from France!"

"There's been a lot to think through." Albert said softly. "You know that."

"I'm just happy to see you." Patrick hugged Albert and then we walked into the sanctuary and sat by him. When the choir approached, and sat in their pews, a wave of comfort wafted over me. Nothing else in the world would feel as good as hearing their music. Patrick whispered to me, "You could always join the choir if you want."

"I'm not a member of the church." I whispered back as the priest walked to the pulpit.

"You don't need to be." he said. "You could try it." He patted my arm.

A bud of hope grew in my chest, and I watched them throughout the mass. Maybe Albert was right about finding a community. Once the mass ended, Patrick escorted me to the man who conducted the choir. "This is a friend of mine, Virginia Crain she's a visitor at the church, and is curious about the choir." Patrick said.

The man shook my head and said, "You're new to this area?"

"No, I've been born and raised here. I was a… a member of a church just down the street,"

"I'm glad to see you here, with Albert, yes?" I nodded. "We have choir rehearsals on Wednesday evenings around six. Usually we have a small potluck beforehand so everyone can eat. You're welcome to join us if you want."

"Thank you," I said.

"I'm Mr. Asher, by the way." He shook my head again and said to the choir, "Good work this morning, good work. I'll see all of you on Wednesday."

Patrick and I walked back to Albert who was standing near the door like he really wanted to leave. "Will you be here on Wednesday then?" Patrick asked me quietly as we approached Oliver.

"I believe so." I said, feeling a bit more confident when the words left my mouth.

"Wonderful, wonderful. I'll be there as well." He shook Albert's hand and said, "Have a blessed Sunday."

When Albert and I returned to his automobile I asked, "Would you mind taking me to choir practice?"

"I would love to." he said, starting the car.

"Why do you go to church if you don't believe it?" I asked.

"I didn't say I don't believe it." he said gruffly. "I don't believe the same things you do. I don't believe in the advent, or the Book of Revelation."

"Why not? It's in the Bible."

He nodded and said, "That it is, but as a historian, it's clear to see that the book is written very colorfully as to safely write to the young generations of Christians who were being persecuted at the time that the Roman empire was going to fall. That's all the book is talking about. It's been interpreted poorly for far too long."

"Perry never said that." I said.

"Because that would probably mean everything he's said to you is false." he said, going through town. "I will see you on Wednesday then. I'm happy you are going to try the choir then, and thank you for joining me for mass. I appreciate it."

Winter was always a time that was nothing more to me than death upon the land. It was cold. It was awful and cruel.

Although I came to believe that God was not much of a cruel being, there were two sides of my mind. One was when it was warm and pleasant, and the other was during winter. Perhaps it always turned me to a living block of ice. My mind turned silent and my body was slow and rigid. I did have a purpose though. I continued with the memory quilt, the cats, and the chickens. To stay warm I ate far more than usual and my mornings, middays and afternoons were filled with hot tea to try to fill me with something better than this pervasive cold that only seemed to fleet away when I was curled up in a ball under a few blankets with a fire and an entire family of cats lying on me.

Snow was a curious thing. Though it symbolized the evil of winter, it was a gorgeous vision of art. The world was blanketed in ice and white snow. The world looked new, fresh, untouched, yet entirely dead. The chickens too were huddled in their coop. They suffered as much as I in the winter months. They became frustrated, bored, and like a parasite, started tearing at their feathers, their best means of warmth, they removed. I hung cabbage in their coop for entertainment purposes. I made toys for them, anything to relieve the stress for them. Opal, still the epitome of stoicness and yet sensitivity, didn't act like the cold or winter bothered her, minus the fact that she burrowed in my bed quilts. I fed her more in the winter to keep her fucntional as well as her growing kittens. I was fearful for them. Opal, though appeared to be doing better than before she had her babies. I saw her walking around with dead mice in her mouth, trotting around proudly. It was during the winter that the mice ran towards the house for warmth and to get out of the wind and near the fireplace. Opal loved the house during the winter. During the summer, she had more room to find food and she'd go through all the fields and the pastures just hoping to find something. Hers was a life I admired and feared.

One could imagine the boredom I experienced if I was thinking philosophically about a cat. I didn't have much else to think about. Clara and George brought me newspapers, but I didn't know if I had the courage to attempt to read them. I knew very little about the world, nor was I good at reading. Even upon reading some and struggling with the words, it seemed like the world was in turmoil. There was constant movement, change. That was how the world worked, yes, it turned. Yet waking up day in and day out and seeing the slightest changes, I often forgot what was happening, what was real.

Chapter Thirteen

Thanksgiving approached and I was communicating very little with my family since the event in mid-September. Clara and George offered that I go to their home within the Brigadier. And upon hearing nothing from Clarence about being allowed to go to my parent's house for the holiday, both Clara and George drove me to their home. Even while in the automobile, I expressed my gratitude, probably to some excessive degree. Their apartment within the hotel was surprisingly spare of belongings although I expected that it'd be very grand, matching the expensive décor of the beautiful establishment. There was nice and comfortable furniture but it was simple. I sat at their couch and relaxed. George brought me warm tea with cinnamon sticks and I was near the fire with a knit shawl around me. I finally felt warm. As much as I tried, I couldn't get my house warm.

On the walls of the parlor room there were high bookshelves filled to the brim with books of all sorts. There were books piled upon the desks. Clara walked in, also holding a tray of porcelain tea cups. "Admiring the collection, ay?" she asked. I nodded in response. "My father was a professor of English at the university. He was a collector of all things in the written word he could find. Since I was little I loved to read, to immerse myself in other worlds."

"Does it work that way?" I asked. "Being so immersed in other worlds?"

"Fictional ones, biographies, really... it's strange. Who would think that reading the ink ridden slides of wood could cause such immense, strange reactions of the mind." She sat down across from me. "I'm currently going through Shakespeare."

"What is that?" I asked, sipping from the spiced drink.

She chuckled a bit and picked up the nearest book from her seat. "He was a very prolific author in the time of Queen Elizabeth the First of England, hundreds of years ago. He wrote a lot of poems, comedies, dramas, tragedies, histories, as well as poetry. He is one of the most important writers ever."

"And which book is that?" I asked.

"Hamlet." she said slowly. "Would you like to read it, Virginia?" She reached to bring to give it to me. I touched the smooth cold leather of the book and opened it then felt the ink bumps on the yellowing pages.

"Thank you." I said. "I will try to read it."

"It is very entertaining, and it'll make you think." She pointed to her head. "It's alright, though, we all need to think sometimes."

"Thinking can be a bit of an issue." I replied quickly.

"Of course, it can." Clara looked to George who walked through the threshold. "Is the turkey finally finished?"

"All carved up and perfect." he responded. As I neared him he said, "It is very nice to have a guest at our house for a holiday."

"Do you not usually have guests?" I asked.

Clara shook her head. "Most of our family is still in North Carolina. We can't leave the hotel long enough to go down there, and most of our family isn't wealthy enough to afford taking the train up here unfortunately." she said. "George and I just never left here after going to university."

"And why did you choose to come to Maine then?" I asked sitting down. Clara poured us some wine. I looked at it suspiciously. The warmth would be welcome; the buzzing feeling would not be.

George looked confused. "I believe it was because I truly wanted to go north."

"So simple." I responded. "It must be different than being trapped in the same place your entire life."

"But your memories get severed." George replied, putting the meat on each of our places. "My childhood is far, far away in my mind. Everything changed once coming into Maine." I'd never eaten turkey before, but it smelled extraordinary. I touched it with the fork.

"Where you two married in North Carolina then?" I asked.

Clara nodded. "Yes. It's surprising how impatient families can be! Seventeen years old. That is preposterous, isn't it? Seventeen years old and married."

George chuckled a bit. "Are you still angry about that?"

"Of course, I am! That was part of my childhood! I could've happily been single a little while longer. If not a long while longer. There was no need to stick me in a white dress and a veil and shove a ring on my finger."

George shook his head. "You were beaming that day."

"So, your memory is clear on that, but just about nothing else." Clara huffed taking a large bite of her turkey. I followed and took a bite. It was juicy but the texture was strange and foreign. It wasn't bad, but I preferred the green bean casserole.

"Why would I forget my wedding day?"

"Because you were eighteen and drunk half the day." Clara responded.

"That isn't correct."

"In your very alcohol clouded mind…" she sighed. "I think I would remember more than you. You weren't paying attention to anything."

"And what makes you think that?"

"Because you were eighteen and drunk." she stated strongly again. "What part about that don't you understand?"

"Possibly we should argue elsewhere…" George muttered, embarrassed by his wife's words. It was entertaining. "Virginia, are you eating well?" George pressed, making brief eye contact.

I chuckled a bit, "You're very stubborn."

"Of course I am. I have to live with her, don't I?" George noted, Clara looking at him with amused shock. "And I'm partially sane too!" He paused for a moment. "Although that doesn't mean either of us can change the subject."

"Yes, I've been eating all of the food." I looked down to my hands which were still long and thin, partially unrecognizable to what they looked like previously. They looked like they belonged to an old woman.

"Well, I hope to see you looking well next time we see you." George said with a heavy sigh. "And we'll be going to town as well. Friday then?"

That evening I spent my time listening to the rustling behind me of Opal and the mewing of her little ones roaming about the house. The windows were open today as it was unnaturally warm. The kittens were standing on the sill, looking out, speaking very loudly. Their eyes were changing colors, and their little bellies sagged in a u-shape. Opal was being a good mother to them. She jumped onto the sill after them, standing carefully above them, soaking in the sun, almost grinning, if cats could grin.

While I was cleaning up the day after Thanksgiving, I came across a loose board on the ground. Beside the kitten size ball of fur, I swept up, it was the only interesting thing I came across. I removed the board. There was a lot of dust forming a cloud and after coughing it away, I peered in. Unable to see hardly I retrieved a candle and held it to the opening. There was a rectangular outline, quite like a book. I reached in and clasped the damp leather. It was red, held together with twine like string. I closed the floor back up and sat in my rocking chair. One of the kittens crawled on my foot and up my skirt and onto my lap. It sniffed the book and grimaced a bit. I opened it up and there was scrawled handwriting: 'Oliver Crain'. As far as I could tell it was a scrapbook, the pages stuck together with age, and were surprisingly fragile. I opened it carefully and there was a photograph of him as an infant. He was dressed in frilly white fabric and was being held by his parents, both of whom were no longer living. Their eyes were bright and staring, their skin surprisingly smooth, almost porcelain. His father looked just as cold and harsh in the photograph as he was in reality. I could remember his booming voice that could roll through the air. All this while his mother showed more joy in this photograph than I'd ever seen in her. She seemed drained her entire life, until her death, her freedom, joy even, was removed from her. I'd never seen her happy.

I questioned what it would be like to grow up amongst such harshness, coldness, stillness. His mother was resigned to his personality, indulging his quirks with the pearls and the cosmetics and the wig. His father whipped him for it. Oliver was confused his entire life. He was still confused now. I never had the ability to be confused until I married him. I was faced with hard realities and expectations and there was no imagining. Now my mind was left to itself and I was forced to imagine conversations between me and Opal, or that there were people walking about my house, invisible to my eyes, or that God was talking to me but I couldn't hear or properly respond. Possibly I was going mad in this house. I was going mad from isolation and silence, and I didn't see an end to it. I just kept continuing on, day after day, morning after morning, night after night. Forever. And I knew that wasn't the truth. Oliver had to return.

Just as expected, a week after Thanksgiving, Clara and George brought me out. The automobile ride in the brisk, iced wind was excruciating but exhilarating. I stuck my head out the window, feeling my lungs constrict, my ears complain with pain, my eyes get cold, my muscles going numb. I held onto my hat and scarf as they wobbled in the wind. I moved my head into the window, shocked by the sudden quiet, despite Clara and George speaking. Clara looked back to me with a smile on her face. "Look at you! A healthy glow finally!"

"I'm not sure being frozen is healthy." I laughed. I laughed. May I repeat. I laughed. It felt foreign and nice. I wrapped my coat tighter around my middle, shivering. There was a smile on my face though, frozen partially also, but there nonetheless, and there for no reason.

Chapter Fourteen

Albert arrived early Wednesday evening. The sound of auto-mobiles became more familiar every week. He approached the house while I finished redoing the braid in my hair. On the kitchen table was some shortbread to share at the small potluck. My heart beat quickly. As with every new thing, I was nervous. I didn't know what to expect, there were new people. Much of my life was within one small community where there were few opportunities for a new start. I pulled my heavy wool coat on to shield myself from subzero temperatures which gripped the land. All of my windows frosted over, and no amount of fire in the fire place or wood burning stove warmed the place up enough. There was no heat in the automobile, and both Albert and I were bundled up tightly, shivering, teeth chattering. My knitted scarf went around my ears but they still felt like they'd fall off, and I thought my feet would never be warm again.

"How is Oliver doing?" I asked quietly.

"He's well, he's well. He's still doing work for the bank, just remotely."

"Will he be home for Thanksgiving?" I asked.

"I don't think so, Virginia. I apologize. Every time I suggest he goes home, he panics. He's also worried that he disappointed you. I let him know the predicament you are in…"

"He has disappointed me." I said. "Let him know that. I'm not going to pretend like everything's alright."

"I didn't expect you to." he said, the engine purring softly beneath us. "He's finally sleeping and eating better. He looks less like the living dead than he did a few weeks ago." As he spoke, I became further angered with Oliver. He didn't have the right to feel such pity for himself while I was suffering as well. He put himself in that situation, and he chose to leave me. He chose to isolate himself in the middle of nowhere. "I hope to return him in better straights than he came."

"It wasn't as if I wasn't taking care of him or feeding him sufficiently enough." I said.

"Once again, I didn't say that."

"What is he wearing?" I asked. "At your house."

"Whatever he likes." he responded bluntly. "I'm not going to stop him."

"Then you're not going to return him in better straights." I said. "That's the entire…"

"Virginia, he's your husband. You should accept him as he is."

"There's a lot of things you're expecting me to accept that are just unacceptable."

"You didn't seem to mind when he told you in the first place." Albert said.

"I'm uncomfortable about all of this."

"It's important that he feels comfortable in my home. He seems to have an affinity for silk… and stockings,"

"Just stop," I said. "I don't need to know."

"Why?"

"Are we going to argue every time we are near one another?" I asked.

"Probably." he said. "At least it's not boring."

"You like arguing with me?" I asked, amused but mostly shocked. He smiled. "This is serious."

"As serious as everything else." He pulled up beside the church. "Do you want me to stay?"

"I can't imagine you singing." I said.

"I sing just fine." he responded. "But that means I'd have to make a commitment to keep joining them."

"You're taking me every week, aren't you? Isn't that a commitment enough?"

"Are you trying to convert me or something?" he asked with a smile.

"That might keep me entertained at least." I said. He turned the automobile off and both of us entered the church. The warmth was welcomed and helped ease my tingling fingers and ears. The smell of food wafted over from a large table in the narthex. I placed my shortbread on the table beside other desserts. Numerous groups of people gathered together in pods around the room discussing while the conductor meandered about. Albert clung to me as much as I clung to Albert until Patrick joined us. He placed his hand freely on my shoulder. I almost jumped out of my skin with the sudden touch, but stayed still. I just wasn't used to it.

The conductor gathered everyone together, encouraging us to hold hands around the long table as he said grace. Immediately afterwards, the place blew up in discussion as people dished out their food. The shortbread cookies I brought were picked up quickly before I got to eat one myself. Albert put a piece of chicken on my plate. "It's good for you." he said jokingly. "You need to get some more meat on your bones."

"You aren't the only one to tell me that." I said jokingly. We got our plates and sat down in an adjacent room and sat at circular tables. Patrick sat beside me with one of his brothers.

"This is Mason," he said, pointing to his brother who sipped his coffee. "He got over here recently."

"Just got a job at the cannery, like everyone else." he said. He smirked at me and said, "Where do you work?"

"I'm a baker. I work for my father's store." I responded. "And a chicken farmer."

"A chicken farmer?" he said with a laugh. "You don't look like a chicken farmer."

"I don't?"

"Too pretty." he said. Heat rushed to my face and I knew I blushed. I smiled and looked down to my feet. Mason turned his eyes to Albert and asked, "What are you?"

"A professor of history." he said bluntly. He hardly touched his food.

"What type of history?"

"Early European history, specifically Western Europe." He stabbed the filet of chicken on his place. I almost flinched thinking that it was a piece of muscle from a once living being. Idly, though, I ate mine, trying to keep myself occupied. "A lot of military history as well."

"Do you think you'll write a book?" Mason asked. Patrick moved his chair a bit closer to me. My body became rigid, but I focused on my food.

"Already have," Albert said.

"You have?" I asked, almost spitting out my food.

"Yes," He sounded confused with my exclamation. "About the tail end of the Viking age in Europe, and the effects of colonization on the British Isles."

"Extraordinary." Mason said. "I can barely read, much less write an entire book." He scoffed at his brother and said, "Neither could he."

The conductor came to the head of the room and said, "About ten minutes before we need to begin! We have a lot of work to do to get ready for Christmas Eve mass! We also need to plan the Christmas bazaar. We'll talk about the bazaar on Sunday, just be ready for that with your ideas for crafts or baked goods. We also have numerous organizations we are looking into donating to but we need to decide upon them. There's a lot to do people. Ten minutes."

Patrick inhaled his food and removed his plate from the table. Albert mutilated the filet of chicken, but it wasn't until now that he ate it. It was clear that all the people in the room were very comfortable and familiar with one another. It was like a massive family, just like the congregation I came from. I ate my food, and slowly we trickled into the large sanctuary and stood in the choir pews. An older man handed out music pamphlets. The song on the top of the pile was "What Child is This". The conductor moved his old wooden stand in front of the choir and flattened out the pamphlet. "This is a new one to our normal Christmas routine, but I just find it so important. We'll begin with just a read through since it's already familiar before we start working out the difficulties."

I felt incredibly ate ease as soon as the song began. Being surrounded by the voices took a hold of me and I knew I found my place. Even when we were stopped frequently to practice specific sections, I found it educational to learn what the different things on the page meant. Considering I could hardly read text, I didn't know how to read music either. Back at the Seventh Day Adventist Church, I only learned the hymns by heart. I could read the words on the page, but the little notes and lines meant nothing to me. The lady beside me, Molly, was an extraordinary singer; she was the choir's best soprano. Shortly after the choir disbanded for the night, I sat down beside her and she pointed out what each of the little notes meant. All the while, Albert was wandering around the sanctuary with his hands in his pockets, looking at the art pieces hanging throughout the location.

Molly said, "I'm sure you'll pick it up over the next few weeks."

"Thank you," I said, smiling. She was around fifty years old. Her hair was short, and thinning with streaks of grey throughout. She powdered her face heavily to try to cover the wrinkles, but it looked fake and made it worse. The mascara on her eyelashes didn't look like they did on Oliver, it looked thicker and clumpy. It was like she dipped her eyelashes in mud. Her cosmetic use didn't stop there, she also had bright red lipstick painted on her lips, and rouge rubbed on her cheeks. At this angle, it looked like a mask, but the voice of this lady was angelic. She was sweet as the dickens. "I'm glad that you are enjoying choir practice," Molly said. "It's nice to see someone new." She hugged me and said, "I hope to see you on Sunday."

"You will." I stood as she gathered her things together. I waved to Albert and he patiently walked over and escorted me out of the sanctuary and to the absolutely frigid vehicle. "You've actually written a book, haven't you?" I asked.

"I wasn't lying," he said with a laugh. "Would you like to read it?"

"I don't think I'd understand anything."

"Don't even want to give it a chance?" he asked with a smile as he turned the automobile on.

"Another friend wants me to read Shakespeare." I said.

"I don't write as complicated as Shakespeare." He chuckled.

The next Wednesday, I met up with a group of women well before choir practice about the Christmas bazaar. Back at my old church, we had numerous bazaars I helped set up, and so I had some experience. I sat near Molly in the circle of old chairs in the narthex of the church. A majority of the women had accents of some sort, whether French or Irish. Molly, though, told me her family had been in the area since the Revolution. One woman with a pad of paper and pencil in her hand said, "Does anyone have anything they've saved up for the fair so far?" There were quilts, hot pads, and wreaths prepared, hidden in people's houses. "Is that all?" she asked. "That's not a lot."

Molly said, "Is there anything we can make in the next few weeks?"

"I can piece together baby clothes, baby blankets," A young woman said. "It's just difficult to put it in the bazaar rather than put it on my own children." Just by looking at her, she didn't look wealthy in the least, but very poor. Her dress was tattered, and there were small holes in her stockings. She was very thin and gaunt.

"Delaney, it is not required for you to-"

"I need to," she said with a sigh. "I should bring at least one thing. There are people out there who need help more than I do." The group fell silent for a little while. Delaney folded her hands on her lap, pressing against her swollen belly. My eyes went straight to her pregnant stomach. In a way I felt both pity and jealousy. Before Oliver left, I truly wanted a child. I wanted to fill my house with laughter, with something that would bring some sort of normalcy, and life. This woman was being burdened with children, when I just wanted to be gifted. "There's no need for worry," she finally added.

"What about baked goods?" the woman asked. "That is the best opportunity we have to bring in money. Seasonal things sell well. Molly, can you make your kringla?"

"Yes, of course." Molly said with a smile. "Always do."

"I'll make gingerbread." Another woman rose her hand. "How much?"

"Plenty," the woman with the pad of paper said. A long list of items I'd never heard of her listed off: pfeffernuse cookies, sugar cookies, brownies, and molasses bars.

"If needed we could always have the hotcake breakfast if needed as well."

I rose my hand nervously and said, "I can bring bread and shortbread cookies." The woman nodded to me and wrote it down before returning to her original topic about the hotcake breakfast. There was discussion about maple syrup and butter, things that were still relatively new to me. The way the women talked though, finishing each other's sentences, gave me a real strong sense of community and hopefulness as well. If I could just be a part of it, I could find a place I belonged.

Albert never gained a sense of comfort. I assumed that was because of the church's view on homosexuality. If they found out about him, they could react in a similar manner as my church did with Oliver. Yet I couldn't help but ask him about my husband. I needed to know. After that Sunday, I invited Albert into my home to eat something. He still stood with his hat in his hands at the door, seemingly uncomfortable. "Would you like something to drink?" I asked.

"All you have is water." he said with a smile.

"Clara and George, friends of Oliver's, they brought over tea. I can get some brewed for you if you like."

"You just want to know how Oliver is doing." he said quietly, rubbing his hands together and putting his hat on the coat stand. "And that's understandable." He joined me at the kitchen table. "I think by winter's end he'll be ready to go back home, or at least I'll make him. I think he's getting too comfortable being away from the rest of humanity. He doesn't have to hide anything." Albert said.

"That long? Until spring?" I croaked.

"That's how long I'm giving him. If he returns earlier, then that's great. I just can't promise it."

I sighed and leaned back in the wooden back chair. "Just tell him what you always tell him for me. Don't go easy on him."

"He's still working and keeps himself busy. I don't let him sit around, idle."

"He doesn't sit around well." I said with a smile. "He doesn't. I will see you again on Wednesday."

The bazaar went well the following week. I brought in a couple dozen shortbread cookies and a dozen loaves of bread. We filled up numerous tables with goods, and it was like half the city showed up to buy things from the women of the church. The money was being donated to veteran's organizations to hopefully help out community members affected by the war. Considering so many of this church's young men went off to war and at least a couple of them didn't return, there was no lack of support here. Albert came as well wearing pieces and parts of his uniform, including his victory ribbon on his chest. I'd never seen him in anything but a gentleman's suit, and it made him look incredibly strange. His entire demeanor changed when he wore the uniform. As stoic and quiet as he usually was, it took another dimension. Other members of the church who were overseas also joined him. They clung to one another with the comradery that came from the war. Nonetheless, we made nearly 300 dollars that day. That was over a quarter of a year's wages, but it still only seemed like a drop in the bucket. Some families lost their father's, or breadwinners. Mothers had to take up work in factories and other jobs just to support their children and to feed them. Some people were still going hungry. The bazaar wasn't enough for the women's group, they wanted to have a food drive to help the working mothers. The women's group here was tireless. Instead of talking about helping, they hardly spoke and just jumped into it. I'd like to think this was truly faith in action, but it also seemed like fulfilling busy work. It was something to consume time, and as I'd been learning here, guilt was something people used like fuel in their work. They believed one had to do good works to get to heaven, and to see God. They also believed that after death a person was judged to go to heaven, hell, or purgatory, the latter being a middling ground where people were purged of their sins before going to heaven. That idea seemed like something Amos Perry would appreciate, but upon asking Albert, he said the idea wasn't in the Bible. He said that the Catholic Church used it since the 1,200s. The Church's tradition was as important as the Bible, which is why Perry had issue with it, and why he called it primitive. Albert claimed that although he wasn't the most religious person on the face of the planet that he accepted the belief that God did not remain silent, and tradition based around a book could be built upon over time. He didn't necessarily agree that it should be led by a man in Italy.

I thought I found my niche, though, and I appreciated being accepted into it by people who used to be strangers. I had a steady routine going with the church, supported by frequent visits by either Clara or George who brought me food. Even though I had access to a store, they were convinced I wouldn't get a nice healthy diet by myself. They treated me like a child. Albert, too, treated me like a child, like I was fragile or breakable. To be honest, though, I felt fragile. I felt like I could break at any moment. The isolation, while interrupted often, was still isolation. While having found a new community, I lost the one I was raised in due to my husband's oddities.

Things, though, never kept their rhythm very long. That was a fact of life. After a long choir practice going over "What Child is This" repeatedly to get the right contonation of the words, all of us were tired, and a little on the cranky side. In the narthex there was fresh coffee being brewed and cookies being eaten. Albert went outside to get some air before bringing the automobile around. It was not too cold of a day. The wind was not brutal, it was hardly existent. Instead there was just the routine numbness of a winter night. I stood against the door, happy to get out of the crowded space. As much as I appreciated company, I was still not terribly adept at handling it in large doses.

I didn't stand there alone very long before Patrick and Mason joined me. Mason was sucking on a cigarette, puffing away. The smell of it was sickening and it felt terrible in my stomach once inhaled. That was one thing I understood about Amos Perry, why we weren't supposed to smoke. Some doctors said it was healthy, but I doubted it. Mason stood on my left and Patrick on my right. Almost immediately I felt incredibly uncomfortable with how close they were to me. They spoke quickly to one another in a thick dialect I couldn't quite understand, and they bumped into my playfully. I forced a smile on my face as not to be difficult, but then Mason put a hand on my shoulder which maneuvered its way into my winter coat, and down towards my breast. I sucked in a deep breath and shuddered. His hand cupped around it tighter and he pressed me against the wall. Patrick made a wall between me and the door to the narthex. Realizing what was happening, I tried to fight against him, but his free hand wrapped around my throat and slammed my head into the wall.

Heat rushed through my ears and into the rest of my body. As much energy was in my body, it temporarily froze.

My body refused to listen to me. "No, no, no…" I repeated, hissing, spitting. They not only ignored me, they did the opposite, and drug me behind the church. One of them began to pull at my coat, undoing the buttons on it and ripping it off my arms. In that instant, I bit Patrick's arm and he yelped, but it only made him angrier, or gave him more energy. He started to hike up my dress. I kicked him best I could, but Mason pushed me down and pinned me in the snowy earth. I kept my legs flailing as much as I could. Patrick positioned himself so his knees were on my legs, keeping them still. I didn't stop flailing though, but my muscles were exhausted. I cried out as loud as I could, hoping someone would listen.

"Virginia?" Albert's voice was small and it felt like it was only carried on the wind.

"Here!" I screeched. "Help!"

Patrick and Mason seemed oblivious to my calls for help. Patrick thrust himself into me and I cried out in pain, but felt defeat almost immediately. He huffed like an animal and used his hands to push my legs further apart. "Virginia?" Albert yelled, and he turned the corner. When he saw Patrick on me, he pulled the man off by his coat and threw him on the ground. Too stunned to move, I just lay there, exposed, cold, and absolutely humiliated. Albert threw Patrick against a wall and started screaming at him until Mason pulled him away. Albert clocked him in the cheek, and blood spewed from Mason's cheek. He then did the same to Patrick, and kicked him in the groin and gut until he was on the ground.

"Come on, let's get you home." Albert said quietly, wrapping his arm around my shoulders, helping me stand. He threw my coat over his shoulder and hurriedly got me to the automobile. I sat on the passenger side, staring ahead. For a moment, everything felt numb and in a blur. Albert started the automobile, but left it idle in the parking lot, looking at me. "Are you alright, Virginia?" he asked. I wished I could have responded, but my mouth was locked shut, and I wouldn't have known what to say. "I honestly never thought those bastards would do something like that." he grumbled under his breath.

As we drove nearer to the house, slowly, all my faculties returned to me. The distinct pain in my groin and my thighs throbbed. I could still feel the hands around my throat. There was a dryness in my mouth. I felt disgusting, like there was filth on every inch of my body. I wanted to wash up desperately, but at the same time I wasn't sure I could move. Once the automobile was parked outside of the house, Albert led me inside, holding onto my hand. I sat down on the rocking chair near the door. He stoked the fire and brought me some water. "How are you feeling?" he asked. I didn't respond. "It's a bad question, I know, sorry. Can you tell me what happened?"

"You saw." I said, my voice just above a whisper. "I tried to stop them... I really... I really did."

He bit his lip and stepped back, shaking his head. "I'm going to-"

"No, no, don't tell Oliver, please. I don't want him to know..." I said.

"Virginia..."

"Please..." I begged. Fear slipped into my veins like acid. I felt like damaged goods, something no one would possibly want now, and if he knew, he wouldn't come back. At the same time, though, I didn't feel safe alone in my own house. "I... can you... can you stay for a little while?"

"Of course." he said, taking a seat on a couch near the fireplace. He noticed the newspaper sitting there beside a copy of *Hamlet* I was slowing making my way through. He read the newspaper quietly while I stared at the ceiling. My intention was to get my thoughts together, but for some time, though, there were no coherent thoughts. My mind just blurred into a mess as I stared blankly ahead. The adrenaline subsided enough I thought I could wash up and get to bed, but as soon as I thought of standing up, the fear entered me again and paralyzed me. The fear was stupid, it didn't make sense. Neither of the men were here, but there was a man. There could be any number of attackers lurking in the dark places.

But there never was before, why would there be attackers there now? Logic didn't seem to have a place in my reasoning. I forced myself to stand and I said, "I'm going to wash up."

"Would you like me to leave?" he asked, not tearing his eyes away from the newspaper.

I didn't know the answer to that question. "I... uh..."

"How about I stay until you're ready to go to sleep?" he asked. I must have agreed because some measure of relief wafted over me, and I nodded. I appreciated his time, and his patience even if his existence was half of my problems. I realized if it wasn't for him, Oliver wouldn't be away, and thus I wouldn't have gone to the Catholic church because I wouldn't have been ostracized from the Seventh Day Adventist community. Yet the man in my living room didn't particularly lead to an angry reaction. He, personally, hadn't done anything to me except... well, sleep with my husband. He was still continuing to do so, and he was going home to Oliver tonight. The thought drilled little holes in my mind as well, only compounding the fear that Oliver wasn't coming back. He must have had something better, something freer with more money, and something that wasn't recently damaged in any way. I was a mess.

In the washroom, I filled the basin with water. The water of course was frigid, but my body's sense of temperature was minimal at the moment. My senses were heightened in other ways. I broke up half a bar of soap and mixed it in there, although I didn't know if it'd be enough to actually rid my body of the filth. With the door closed, I removed my clothing. All I had to see by was a few small candles, and a mirror. There were already defined marks on my thighs. I scrubbed in my groin area, making sure nothing remained. It was already bleeding there due to the force. I kept wiping up the blood, fretting over how it was in my clothing and bloomers as well.

I sat on the floor of the bathroom, staring ahead at the wall again. It seemed to be the only thing to keep my mind quiet, but it kept scrubbing and wiping. I didn't know how long I was in the bathroom before I changed into my nightgown. I didn't want Albert to see me in my sleeping clothes, so I only put my head out the door and said, "Albert, I'm going to sleep. Thank you for staying for a while."

He stood up and turned towards me. The fire continued to burn in the fireplace, sending some warmth my way. "Are you sure you're alright?" he asked.

"I never said I was." I muttered.

"I apologize for what happened,"

"You didn't do it." I interrupted.

"I should have stayed by you, escorted you."

"Usually I'm quite fine on my own." I said, crossing my arms. At least in some way he was safe, I could trust him. He had no interest in me like the Irish men at the church.

"I'll check in on you in a few days. Would you like to go to the police or anything?"

"No." I said. "I... I don't want to cause any more trouble."

"You didn't cause the trouble, Virginia." He pressed. "Patrick and Mason did, and they should be punished for what they did."

"I said I'm not going to the police. I'm… I'm just going to go on like normal."

"You don't want to go back there do you?" he asked.

"I… no, no, no," I said. "Good night."

And in that day, I lost the second community I'd been adopted into. I couldn't go back there and face them. I could only imagine the sly looks on their faces, the smirks. Even if I stayed close by Albert, I couldn't trust that I would be safe. I'd never encountered such violence before. Mother always said things happened for a reason, but I felt like this was a punishment. Maybe Reverend Perry was right, what I was doing was wicked, and I needed to be punished for it. Why was it me though?

Spring was extremely welcome after a lonely, empty winter, with no formal Christmas, nor any other of the fixings of the holiday season. I learned to move on with life as best as one can when there are traumas that loom in the back of one's mind. I did have somethings to keep my occupied. The kittens grew and were partially independent adolescents. I was careful to keep them healthy and plump. Opal was drifting further and further away from them, back into her normal routine.

I was outside on the first day of March feeding the growing flock of chickens. It was a little windy and drizzly this day, the sky churning with a thick foggy grey color. The wind was chilled but had a hint of humidity to it, suggesting that the winter was coming to an end. The chickens were still fluffed up, acting heavy and bored. Even such a small brain as a chicken's could get stressed. I hung root vegetables from the ceiling of their coop to keep them occupied. Now that it was a bit warmer, I could let them out to forage. They were able to stretch their legs, and get to pecking at the ground.

There was the clicking of familiar horses' hooves coming up the street. I expected it to be Clarence coming to pick up the eggs early, and I didn't move. The basket was set on the porch filed to the brim with eggs gathered this morning. My eyes were heavy and I didn't have much energy to face anyone at the moment. Clarence was still my brother, and still acted as such. He was protective, but now he was confused. I don't think he knew how to act with me having been affiliated with someone so… against nature, against God. Supposedly that was what Oliver was, compatriots with the devil or something. Clarence never mentioned it really, but his facial expressions and eyes suggested it, and with the passing weeks he probably thought that I was becoming some sort of witch or recluse. I didn't like to be approached our touched, in fact it made my skin crawl with a feeling of filth.

The cart came to a stop and I turned around briefly, expecting Clarence's basic greeting of "Hello, I'm here to pick up the eggs" followed by a comment about the weather. It wasn't Clarence, but Oliver. I stood up straight and continued to peer over, trying to adjust my sight to see if the image would change. Yet Oliver still sat there on the seat of the cart, hands still holding the reins and a very small smile on his face. He nodded to me cordially. I wiped my hands on the apron wrapped around my waist and jogged over. Elation flooded through me at that instant, I wanted to jump up there and hug him so tightly he'd break, but something stopped me.

He looked down at me and touched my cheek sweetly. I didn't know what to say, but my heart was flitting around in my chest, both confused and happy and a multitude of other emotions. He stepped down from the cart and embraced me. I hadn't felt an embrace in months in any sort of way. I hugged him tightly and buried my head in his chest, feeling him breathe and his heart beat. We made eye contact for a while, his eyes shaking slightly. He kissed my cheek and put his hands on my face kindly again. Still with no words I followed him into the barn with the cart and released the horse into the pasture.

We went inside and sat at the kitchen table, staring at one another. Neither of us dared to speak. In the silence of the bright morning, Opal jumped onto the table and stood between us, her tail high in the air. She looked at us like we were the mad ones and sat down. I smirked a bit at her actions. The kittens followed beneath the table, swarming Oliver, exploring him as a new person. Opal eyed him suspiciously, and rightfully so.

"Would you like anything to eat?" I asked, breaking the silence for the sake of hearing his voice.

For a brief moment in the quiet, I anxiously waited, hoping that his voice would be as a remembered it. "I would love something to eat." he responded. I retrieved him some muffins baked with fruit preserves I was going to eat as breakfast this week. "Thank you." he quietly responded. "How are you Virginia?"

"Would you like the truth?" I asked honestly, feeling heat swell in my chest. He didn't respond. "Quite badly actually. Since you left me here, alone, I have not hardly spoke to anyone except for Clara and George, and I am thankful for them, but... I have been utterly ostracized from my family, from everything I know."

"I wish none of this ever happened..." he breathed. "I'm so sorry, Ginny, I truly am... I never meant to harm anyone."

"I know you didn't, but that's what happened." I crossed my arms and leaned against the chair. "Am I allowed to ask what happened while you are away?"

He took a bite out of the muffin and stood up to get the butter sitting on the counter. He sat back down before saying anything. "I was just trying to find answers, Ginny."

"About what?"

"About myself."

"That's specific…" I muttered unhappily.

"Do you think we could… just pretend this never happened?" he asked.

"Are you trying to be realistic? Oliver, we've both changed so much…" I looked around uncomfortably, feeling antsy, restless. "I don't know what happened while you were gone, and you seem to unwilling to tell me. I thought you said we weren't going to hold secrets. This isn't a way to conduct a marriage."

"No, it's not." he said. "It never was." He hadn't eaten any more of the muffin after he put the butter on it.

"That's what I want though. I just want to be normal, to be in a marriage like everyone else, except maybe happy. I'd like to be happy actually." I huffed. "The other day I thought it was strange that I laughed. Oliver, that's not alright."

"I'm sorry, Ginny…" he breathed, his voice hardly reaching me through the space in the air.

"I know you are." I stood up from the chair and went to the bedroom to finish up making the bed. Oliver stood in the doorway and watched me. I wanted to ignore that he was there. I was happy for a few minutes, now I was still unfortunately frustrated with Oliver, and I didn't know why.

That night was no better. I was staring at the ceiling. Oliver was so tired that he fell asleep almost immediately after hitting the pillow. His breath slowed and became even. He lay flat on his back, as did I. I wasn't used to there being someone beside me again. It was a bit comforting though knowing he was there. He was safe, and so was I, but it was still difficult to sleep. I woke late in the morning after a myriad of strange dreams to the smell of something baking. I opened my eyes to see Oliver walking in with a tray with caramel rolls and fruit. He had a bright smile on his face and placed it over me. "How does it look?" he asked proudly.

"Very nice," I responded with a smile. "Thank you, Oliver."

"I thought you'd like it. You always did have quite a sweet tooth." He watched me with attentive eyes. I accepted it, finishing up the breakfast quickly, my stomach stretched with the food. It hadn't been that way in a long way, especially with not a warm sweet meal, especially on a Sunday.

"Would you like to go on a walk with me?" I asked finally, breaking another silence after taking a large final bite of the dwindling caramel roll. His face spread with joy.

"I'd love to."

I got out of bed and put on an old dress and my heavy boots. He looked concerned at my appearance. He placed his wide brimmed hat on his head and placed his hands in his jacket pockets. "Are you ready?" I asked.

"Am I?"

We went through the pasture to the deep forest following my favorite, now familiar path. I just loved being so comfortable amongst the canopy and the emerging leaves of the woods. Oliver held onto me tightly, protectively as if I was going to fly away. I just wanted to sit on some rocks and listen to the sound of the birds singing, but I wanted to share it with him. The birds were distant for the entire winter as well. I felt alone without their noise, and in the forest, they were at their freest, although birds always seemed to be quite free. As we sat on the flat stones, he reached over to kiss me. I was startled by his actions but not entirely unhappy about it. He was urgent, but gentle, one hand resting on my stomach. He pulled away and rested his forehead against mine. "I missed you, Ginny."

I nodded, and looked away. It was his own decision to leave, his own decision to be apart from me. It amazed me how angry I could be. I clasped his hand in mine and kissed it. "I still love you Oliver."

He smiled brightly and nodded. "I love you too."

Chapter Fifteen

We adjusted to life as it was before. Oliver returned to work, but I didn't. I stayed at home much to my disgrace baking and gathering eggs for the store. I wished to return to work as well, to leave the house and be back around people. I liked being able to take home money at the end of the week or month, knowing that I did my part to help my family. Yet the only help I could provide was to increase the flock of chickens, continuing to provide food for my father and brother's store. Clarence seemed very interested that Oliver returned, but didn't ask any questions. I didn't ask questions either. It was better for us just to remain silent.

I returned to eating good meals, even though I thought I lost a taste for it. I made roast chicken and duck quite often, mixing it with well herbed vegetables. There were different sweet breads that I tried making. That was one change that was whole heartedly embraced- that of honey, sugar, meat, and savory seasonings.

One morning shortly after getting washed and dressed for the day Minnie came bumbling into the house carrying a heavy box of cookbooks. I sat at the table with my morning tea and toast, exhausted from a long night without sleep. Opal kept me up all night with her meowing. Honestly, I just wanted to be in bed at the moment, but Minnie immediately began talking with her bright and gentle voice. "Good morning, Virginia. I went through Sally's things and thought that you might be interested in some of her cookbooks. There are some interesting things here. Maybe you can get some serious use out of these." She placed the box on the table and shook her head, wiping off sweat. "I really don't know how paper can get so heavy. Really, it's strange." It'd been months since I'd seen, much less spoken to her. Her arrival was sudden.

She lifted up a book and said, "This one is just bread, just bread. Look at this." She placed it next to me and sat down. "You're quiet, haven't said anything."

"I don't think you've given me a chance to." I said with a smile, picking up the old book. The paper was rough and old, some of it was fragile enough that it could break under pressure. "This molasses bread looks wonderful." I pointed to a recipe I turned to.

"Get some weight on you too." Minnie said, patting my back with some pressure.

"Is that all you think about?" I laughed. "I think it will taste good."

"You know I was trying some of this at home, and I take some of it to the shelter I've been working with. There's an herb bread in there, a buttermilk bread, chocolate even. Who ever heard of chocolate bread? A little on the expensive side, but just think about it for like a holiday or something."

"I know it's far away from Thanksgiving, but… can I be there?" I asked.

"What do you mean, dear?" she asked. My voice was so quiet when I spoke, I wasn't sure she heard me.

"No one spoke to me for the holidays this past year…" I said. "Do you think that we could have the holidays together now?"

"You know, Virginia, I wanted you there this year. I really did." she said sincerely, closing the book. "It was everyone else…"

"And by that you mean?" I began.

"Your parents. You understand…"

"Only a little." I said with a sigh.

Minnie took in a deep breath before hugging me. "I want everything to be back to normal, Virginia. I don't know if it will be though… after all that's happened."

"The preacher seeing my husband in a dress? That's all he saw. That's all he knows."

She whispered, "Amos Perry knows that your husband is…. A homosexual."

"A homosexual? Oh my…" I put the other books back in the box. I was trying to pretend that was absurd, a lie.

"You still love him though, don't you?"

"Why wouldn't I?" I asked, concerned. As I said that, Oliver walked in.

"Hello, Ginny, Minnie, I have the groceries." he said quietly, closing the door before Opal jumped outside. He put the paper bag on the table. He handed me some flowers before kissing my cheek. Minnie watched him suspiciously, her entire body tensed up.

"Why aren't you at the bank today?" I asked.

"I have the day off, they're doing renovations in the building. I thought that we could spend some time together today." he said quietly.

Minnie suddenly said, "Well, this morning maybe you could help us try some of these recipes." Minnie stood up and patted his back as well. Oliver smiled and chuckled. I let out a sigh of relief.

"Sounds good, sounds good."

"You aren't supposed to eat half the things in this book." I said with a smile.

She shrugged. "It isn't going to kill me." She opened the book and asked, "What do you want to start with? You don't happen to have coco powder, do you?"

"Oh no, definitely not." I said. She searched in her bag for a small notepad.

"I should pick some of that up next time we meet up. The idea of chocolate bread intrigues me."

"I think I have the ingredients for the buttermilk herb bread." I said, flipping through until I landed on the page.

"Then there's the Russian black bread. That looks really good too." Minnie said.

"We can always make both." I said. "It's not like they won't get eaten."

After our interesting baking marathon, I gave her the memory quilt that was hanging on a quilt rack in my living room. Her smile was so welcome, as was her warm hug. She didn't treat me like I was a stranger, or a hermit. That's all I needed at the moment, to be treated like a human.

The books contained plenty of things to keep supper interesting over time. Oliver and I were practically force feeding ourselves to get all the food eaten in time.

That night while we were preparing for bed, I sat on Oliver's side of the bed. He approached me and kissed my forehead. "What are you thinking about?" he asked. "I can see the gears working in your head."

"I think it's time we think about having children." I said, sitting cross legged.

"You think we're ready?" he asked, throwing the hand towel over his shoulder.

"We're doing well right now. If we keep up like this, yes." I responded. "We've been married nearly a year."

"In retrospect, honey, that's not that long."

I sighed and added, "Oliver... this decision is as much yours as it is mine, but I'm more than ready."

"To be a mother?"

"Yes. I think a child could do us good, help us be normal."

He smiled and shook his head. "That's not what children are for, Ginny."

"You know what I mean." I pressed, grabbed his hand.

"Alright," he agreed. Up until this point we weren't having intercourse in any regular interval. At first with his return, both of us were uncomfortable with one another for any number of reasons, and we still hadn't gotten a working rhythm between the two of us. Oliver said it'd take practice, and trying for pregnancy was our opportunity. It was good for us to learn to be closer to one another, and to learn to live in the moment. Neither of us were good at the latter part. We were always looking every direction but at the one we were actually in.

It wasn't long before I was convinced I was pregnant.

Soon after discovering this, Minnie had visited me while Clarence was too busy at the store to retrieve the eggs for the store. She hugged me as she did the previous time and put her hands on my cheeks. She was one of the few people I was related to who did not treat me like I was a contagious piece of sin. "Look at you! You look wonderful! Beautiful too!" She giggled a bit and bid me to sit with her on the porch swing, holding my hand. It was a relief to just be around her. "How are you feeling Virginia?" The sky appeared to be giving up winter once and for all and the wind was warm and smelled sweet, not just cold and bitter.

"A little odd, actually. I think I may be with child, but I don't know."

"Have you missed bleeding?" she asked. I nodded. "And have you felt a bit ill?" I nodded as well. "Are you feeling sore?"

I nodded again. "Well, you should see a physician to know for sure. You'll need to take care of yourself really well, to keep this baby you might be carrying and yourself healthy and alright. I'm very happy to hear the news."

"Please, don't share it with anyone." I responded quietly.

"It's good news though! Why wouldn't you want your family to know?"

"They don't deserve to know; the way they have treated me." I answered heatedly, avoiding eye contact. I didn't want to see the hurt in her eyes.

"Unfortunately, I agree with you. I should leave soon. If I take too long, Clarence will ask questions."

I still felt different though despite many things getting better. Ever since I'd been what could only be described as abandoned, and the attack, something was wrong. My mind was clouded, heavy, and my memory wasn't functioning properly. I was incredibly restless. I tried to keep up with myself, and the farm. I wanted to be normal, like Oliver and I promised each other we would be. Although, daily I questioned the possibility, accepting it might not happen anymore. Stubbornness might just have to be a quality I invest in. This child that was growing inside me needed a proper family, a mother who was available. A mother better than the cold, distant, straight-laced, unhappy mess I was granted.

And that gave me some hope, and fear. The fear was purely of the unknown. I was never allowed to know how this worked, a child growing within me, only how it came to be, and that was hardly discussed as well. There was no information on how a union could produce something so small that would eventually grow large, get a soul, and be born, then develop into a fully functioning human being. Pregnancy wasn't safe, that much I did know. I was warned by my mother on many occasions about women who died in labor, or the child being born dead. There were complications that led to heavy bleeding, and dangerous infections. There were so many things that could go long that no one could count, and only God could know. She liked to fill me with fear about things like that. In this case, she wasn't going to be aware of this until I was showing, and I attempted to return 'home'. The word home was a battered word. I wasn't sure what it meant anymore.

Slowly, this house was becoming home for me. Home was never where I resided, but it was different, there was a feeling attached to it. It was the feeling of being safe. Now that all was well. I felt safe. I knew all the walls, and they knew me. I was welcome. And now it was becoming a wonderful place to be, despite this awful feeling that continued to pollute me. Clara and George still came over regularly, and I cooked for them. That was all I could do to connect myself to others. They were bright, colorful people, and spent as much time as they could at our house on evenings they joined us. I tried strange types of chicken dishes, egg dishes, and strange breads, like the chocolate bread. We were all surprised by how savory the bread was, rather than the sweetness we expected. Buttermilk herb bread was Oliver's favorite. I just enjoyed bringing some happiness, even if it was just through food.

For one of our dinner parties with Clara and George, I spent almost every hour since I work this morning in the hopes to get everything completed for it. The china was cleaned and shined, the crystal glasses were brought out and candles were set up throughout the house to clean up the stench of dust and cats. I wanted something different today, to feel put together, and I was going to cook some lemon spiced chicken. Oliver went to the grocery in town to get some lemon juice to use on the chicken on his way home from work. I marinated the fresh meat with the garlic spice mixture. I made a mash with sweet potatoes, red potatoes, carrots, and peas. Just looking at the food made me hungry, especially when I went on making a good chocolate cake, and bread with a beautiful thick crust. Everything in the meal would work together well, at least I hoped so. I wasn't a chef, but I knew what tasted good.

I paced around the kitchen with my good calico dress on and warm stockings. "What are you worrying about?" Oliver said, placing his hand on my shoulder to stop the pacing.

"I don't know," I responded with a laugh. "I really, really don't know."

"It smells wonderful, it looks wonderful. They'll appreciate the gesture." Oliver kissed my ear. I put my hand on his neck and hugged him.

"Thank you. You're always supportive."

"Although I can't cook worth anything." Oliver said.

"I know, last time you tried to cook dinner, I wasn't actually sure what I was eating."

"Yeah… I tried." he said, shaking his head. "And I burn everything. I'm too optimistic about how much time is remaining."

"That's why you watch the clock, it helps." I still paced around, feeling like there was something crawling under my skin. The automobile came clicking up the road, puttering along. It sounded so unstable, and sounded like a monster going to sleep when George turned the car off. He stood up partially and waved at us from the open top. They always looked so perfect and clean. George wore a nice flat hat and glasses to protect his eyes. It was clear that Clara hadn't given up on trying to make him more fashion-forward. He opened the door for Clara who stepped out gracefully, kissing his cheek. Any sign of physical affection between the two was a rare sight to see. Clara usually treated George more like a brother than a husband, but George didn't ever appear to have issue with it. I didn't see what happened behind closed doors.

They hardly ever knocked anymore these days and just walked right through. "Good evening!" George said, hanging Clara's coat up on the rack.

"It smells wonderful in here!" Clara said, hugging me. "Lemon chicken is it?"

"How'd you know?" I replied, stepping up to them. George patted Oliver's shoulder with some force.

"George's favorite."

"Come on in, George!" Oliver said as he returned to the living room.

"Have you read Hamlet yet?" Clara asked. The book was sitting on a small table next to the rocking chair.

"Yeah…" I said. "It was difficult." I was about half way through it when the attack happened. Reading slowed down even further after that. In some ways, I connected the story to the attack.

"Never said it was easy." Clara said, sitting down at the table. "George, why are you still standing over there! Be polite."

"I am being polite…" George muttered, walking over with Oliver. He yawned and sat down beside his wife.

"But what did you think, Virginia? About the book, I mean."

I brought out the lemon chicken and mash and placed it on the table. The dining room was lit up by many large candles and some lamps. "That poor Ophelia girl, lost her mind… over some horrible boy."

"They were in love." Clara said.

"Didn't look anything like love to me." I said. "Hamlet wasn't nice to her, he was downright rude, and she just took it. At first, though, I thought she was pretending to be insane, but then she ended up in the river."

"Don't think foul play could have been involved?" Clara asked with some light in her eyes, smirking.

"I didn't think about that... the book didn't look into that." Oliver and George looked at each other from across the table, looking amused. "I think they're smarter than us." I said to Oliver.

"Oh I know they are." Oliver added with a small laugh, cutting into the chicken. "Only thing I'm good for is working numbers."

"That's your job." I said, kissing his hand. "You're good at what you do. That's what matters."

"Neither of us are very bookish people." Oliver said. "It's new."

"She had to do something, Oliver, with her time." Clara said sternly, her eyes expressing something like anger towards Oliver. It was the first time she even mentioned it since he returned. Up until this point, she walked on eggshells, like all of us.

"I apologized to everyone for this already..." Oliver said, closing his eyes, leaning back uncomfortably in his chair.

"I know," I said. "This is supposed to be a nice dinner."

Apparently, that was a difficult idea to grasp at any one moment. Such a large hole in the past year could not be patched up so quickly, nor did any of us fully understand the necessity. Personally, all I wanted was to eat and have comfortable conversation, and I would press for that to happen and continue to happen. "It is," George said with a smile.

Clara chuckled and said, "He doesn't appreciate my cooking."

"What cooking?" he asked with a laugh. "You only do that on special occasions. The rest of the time I'm left to my own devices, and I can't even properly make cream of wheat."

"It's not supposed to be a brick, George." Clara said. "If you would just follow the directions…"

"You make it sound so easy!" he exclaimed.

"It is…" she said, clearly amused and yet frustrated. "That and there's a perfectly fine kitchen right in our building. They make wonderful food."

"How is the hotel doing?" Oliver asked.

"It's growing." George said. "We've been hiring quickly to keep up with everything. You know that."

"I just know the books." Oliver said with a smile.

"We're bringing in all sorts of acts, sideshows, lectures, music acts. Since we're about the only place for entertainment, we've been able to do whatever want." George said. "It's extraordinary really. We've been saving up all the advertisements for our shows. I'm hoping over time our hotel will become an attraction to bring people from further away."

Clara said, "Lectures have been something new though, educational lectures with professors and academics from all over talking about their field of research. It's giving us a bit more respect than the vaudeville shows, as much as George enjoys those…"

"Wait a minute," George interjected. Oliver laughed and looked to his plate. "Those lectures were my idea."

"No, no, no, remember I was reading that book about Lincoln, and I mentioned that there were people going around giving lectures and they drew a crowd."

"And I was the one that arranged the first one, the professor of medicine, remember?" George pressed. "You just talked about it, you didn't do anything about it."

"It was my idea though," Clara said, crossing her arms. She then turned to me and said, "They are truly impressive. You ought to come by and see some of the lectures with us.

We like to see as many as we can since we're the ones paying for them to come."

While Oliver and I were lying in bed the next morning, both of us were reluctant to move as we were far too comfortable. He turned to me and placed his hand on my belly. I smiled a bit and kissed his arm. He chuckled. "One day we might become a bickering old couple like Clara and George." I said.

"Is that what you want?" he chuckled.

"They don't fight with one another. They just are around each other too much." I laughed. "They finish each other's sentences. How long have they been married?"

"Fifteen, sixteen years?"

"I wonder what we'll have in that many years." I said. "Where we'll be."

"Probably not owning a fancy hotel." He chuckled. "I don't want to be a chicken farmer forever."

"You work in finance, though." I said. "At the bank."

"Yes," He lay down, stretching his arms up, clearly comfortable.

I placed my hand on his chest, feeling the soft flannel. It moved unnaturally on his skin. Confused I unbuttoned the shirt a way and saw part of my dress slip. I sighed heavily and removed my hand quickly. Ashamed, he quickly buttoned his shirt back up. I didn't want to say anything but fear and disappointment filled me to the brim. He was returning to the madness that plagued us before. I turned away before closing my eyes and got out of bed. "Ginny?" Oliver whispered.

"Don't do it again." I hissed.

"Ginny…" he muttered. "No one sees it. It's… it's just for me."

"You're mad." I replied quickly, heatedly. The pain that crossed his face hurt me more than finding the satin under his shirt. I sighed and melted a bit. I stepped up to him and added, "I shouldn't have said that. Please, though, Oliver, you're scaring me." He bit his lip and nodded, but said nothing. The slip didn't return to my dresser.

Throughout the hot summer, we both found ourselves relaxing on the pond out near the forest. Oliver had bought a small row boat so we could float on the water. I loved being amongst the sounds of the insects and the frogs. The plopping of fish breathing, and Oliver humming hymns we both knew. He liked to fish, but he never kept hardly anything he caught. He loved eating fish, but I didn't, and so once in a while it was a treat for him. "Catching anything?" I asked.

"I think you'd notice if I brought a fish in." he said with a smile. "I'm going to try over by the falling willows."

"You're not getting anything. Sun's too high. Why don't you take a break?"

He sighed and brought the pole in. This was a time we could be together, outside of the home and confines, and securely out of the eyes of anyone. Despite the heat, I leaned back against his chest and he wrapped his arms around me. I looked ahead into the powder blue sky, watching some cottony clouds pass by. The constant sounds of life were calming, the bugs, the birds, a heron or two, and the wind in the leaves. It reminded us how small and connected we were. He kissed my cheek and I smiled. "I love you." he said.

I moved around slightly and said, "I love you too."

The summer was coming to end, though, very soon, and I remembered my situation this time last year, and I felt heavy again. There were brief moments of lightness, and brief elation, but as mentioned, they were few and far between. Now knowing that it'd soon be cold and desolate again made me feel utterly wretched. It'd just lead me into thinking of things I lost. Things I'd rather forget, and push away in the recesses of my mind. Oliver and I spent as much time outside as we could before that happened, even as it began to feel chilled and the land around us died.

I began to show just a little bit, with a hard, round bump forming on my belly. I stood in front of a mirror hanging in the washroom. There'd never been a bump there before, and especially never one that looked so unnatural and foreign. Right around my hips it looked like I ate too much. Oliver stepped behind me and put his hands on my belly and kissed my cheek. When his hand curved around the bump the baby moved, quite a lot actually, to let us know that it was in there. This wasn't the first time I felt the baby, at times in the night I'd wake to unexpected movement. How this baby managed to fit in there, grow in my belly, I still didn't know. My plan was once I was big enough for people notice a bit more, I would venture back to church. Oliver was willing to join me, as if it was proof to confirm that he was a reasonable husband.

With a few more weeks of Oliver and I getting courage enough to reenter into society while letting my stomach grow, on Saturday morning, we dressed in our best clothes and drove the cart down the familiar road to church. As we bounced along the rutted road, wrapped tightly in my shawl, I thought of how many times we'd done this in the past. In a way, things settled in my mind back to the way things used to be. The church hadn't changed a bit since the last time I saw it. It was still a simple white rectangular building surrounded by flat grassland, right on the edge of town. There were carts already hitched up front and people walking inside. Oliver put his hat down further as if to avoid eye contact. I put my hand on his leg for some support, although this would be difficult for the both of us. It had been over a year since we were last here. Hopefully the time and space was beneficial. We were going to have to face some difficult problems today. I kept telling myself to be brave, over and over, and over again.

We entered the doors and there was some silence, quite familiar to that of the last time we'd been to this place. Last time, Oliver ran out of here in the middle of the sermon. I hadn't felt this nauseous in a long time. My brother looked up, startled to see me. Minnie's face beamed though with something resembling pride. I wanted to cling to her for courage. I stepped up to them, with all the courage I already possessed, holding sternly onto Oliver's face. There were eyes going almost immediately to my belly, and then my eyes. "Good morning," I said to them, acting as if there had been no disparity between us. "Would you mind if we joined you?"

"I think that would be lovely," Minnie said. "Don't you think, Clarence?"

Clarence looked like he wanted to agree, but he then looked to our parents for encouragement. My father nodded, heavily sighing. Clarence's face, flushing with relief. I hadn't seen such kindness in his eyes for a long time. Father eyed Oliver again and we went inside the sanctuary and sat at our regular pew. It was so familiar I could feel my back stiffen into perfect alignment. The whispering was the same as last time; it was the whispering that usually pervaded any small community. They had very little else to speak about but anything that could be considered different, and as much as I wished it wasn't true, Oliver was different and they had evidence that he was a deviant, even if that was but Amos Perry seeing him in a dress once.

Amos Perry stepped up to the pulpit. He looked more terrifying than usual with his eyes bearing down on us, glassy and
dark. He swayed from side to side, waiting for the sanctuary
to fall completely silent. "Good morning brothers and sisters
in Christ Jesus." he began. His eyes kept returning to Oliver
and I. "I just wanted to thank everyone who participated in
the hospital visits this past week. We have been welcomed back
again. The Thursday night dinner was also quite successful. We
are making a community worthy of God's gaze, and worthy of
the remnant church, but we can do better. As it says in the book
of Galatians: Bear one another's burdens and so fulfill the law
of Christ. It is desperately important to build a world worthy
of Christ's return. We must spread the gospel, the good news,
and bring people within the folds of the church. In Hebrews
it says: And let us consider how to stir up one another to love
and good work, not neglecting to meet together as is the habit
of some, but encouraging one another, and all the more as
you see the Day drawing near." Reverend Perry's words were
surprisingly soft. "The Day is coming, as we have been waiting.
And we must hold fast together. Two are better than none,
because they have a good reward for their toil. For if they fall,
one will lift up his fellow. But woe to him who is alone when
he falls, and has not another to lift him up! Again, if two lie
together, they keep warm, but how can one keep warm alone?
And though a man might prevail against one who is alone, two
will withstand him- a threefold cord is not quickly broken." He
stepped away from the pulpit and stood before us. "We must
hold fast together, keeping each other up. We must keep each
other, hold each other. In Thessalonians it says and we urge you
brothers, admonish the idle, encourage the fainthearted, help
the weak, be patient with them all." He grinned and looked
across the entirety of the congregation. "And patience is one of

our greatest virtues, pulling us through all, keeping us humble, eager, and ready. All the while holding us accountable for our actions. Therefore, you must confess your sins to one another and pray for one another, that you may be healed. There is power in honesty, and truthfulness. It allows what Paul says, to let love be genuine. You must abhor what is evil, hold fast to what is good. Love one another with brotherly affection. Outdo one another in showing honor. Do not be slothful in zeal, be fervent in spirit, serve the Lord. Rejoice in hope, be patient in tribulation, be constant in prayer. This will pull you through all things until the end. And if we walk in the light, as he is in the light, we have fellowship with one another and the blood of Jesus his Son cleanses us from all sin".

"But you are the chosen race, a royal priesthood, a holy nation, a people for his own possession, that you may proclaim the excellency of him who called you out of darkness into his marvelous light. Once you were not a people, but now you are God's people, once you had not received mercy, but now you have received mercy." Perry stepped into the center of the aisle and continued to turn to make eye contact with us all. "You must understand your importance on the face of this earth. You were placed here with purpose. You were formed to assist the world, to give, not take. To follow the laws given, and keep the peace."

He fell silent and walked away from the pulpit as the piano began to fill the emptiness. We proceeded to sing some hymns, all of which I heard so much in my life that I had them memorized. Oliver's voice beside me was incredibly comforting though. He sung well, his voice was smooth but crackled a few times. I stood incredibly tall, feeling as time went on more courage than before, almost defiance, even though I did not feel welcomed or comfortable. The situation was laughable in a way.

After the singing of hymns and the offering collection, Oliver and I walked out into the narthex, peering back as people began to clump together in groups to talk. I felt I was not welcomed to the lady's group today, however it could always be quite a curious event, even an adventure. But when it was clear that no one was going to approach either Oliver or I, we decided to leave.

Oliver was silent while he was driving the cart. "That wasn't that bad." I said quickly.

He nodded but asked, "Do we have to do that again? That was excruciatingly long."

"You'll live." I said.

"Sure, sure, as long as they don't get their hands on me, I'll live. I don't think they've forgotten anything over the time."

I shook my head and said, "Let's be positive please."

"Positive… I'm not sure how well I can do that."

So that little bit of happiness I'd been building up for months was beginning to dwindle. "You have no strength sometimes, Oliver. You crumble under pressure." He didn't respond, just urged the horse faster. "Oliver, don't ignore me."

"I'm not." he quietly said. "However I'm not a fan of being insulted."

"It's criticism, meant to be constructive. You need to face things like this. You can't just hide, or runaway, especially now that we are expecting a child."

He was silent again. Even in the event that he needed to respond intelligently, he refused to speak.

Chapter Sixteen

Oliver was only comfortable at home, and there we worked together well. It was the only place on earth we were both comfortable. There was no visible frustration or anger on my part, although he continued to act like a beaten puppy. I wasn't sure if he would ever recover from the realization people knew he secret. I thought through all the words Reverend Perry said; that we should strive for greatness, and forgiveness, to assist those around us. No one in that church listened to those words. No one approached us to say hello, to greet us, nor did they act like we were anything but vermin. The other part of his sermon, I already understood well, I didn't particularly like being idle. It was frustrating, and so I worked. Although my father still wasn't asking me to return to work at his store, and the orders he placed with me were dwindling as well. I hoped I could find something else to do with my time, even in the event of my child's birth in a few months.

Minnie now felt free to visit a great deal now, and we would sit outside on the benches or the porch swing while it was still nice outside. She always had a calm smile on her face, and interest and happiness in her eyes. We had a similar frame of mind when it came to appreciating the weather to its fullest extent. "I'm going to go to the shelter tomorrow, would you like to join me?" she asked.

"Do you think Clarence would mind?" I asked.

"It doesn't matter if he minds it." Minnie said defiantly. "You deserve to do what you think is right. It seems that no one listens to Reverend Perry's sermons." I sighed and nodded in agreement. "We're supposed to support one another, not run away in fear because of something we don't understand."

"Yes, but they've also been taught to avoid evil, and if they think something is going against God, they are supposed to avoid it at all costs." I replied.

"Yes, but one commandment should be more important than the other." she said with a flighty voice. "Are you interested then in coming with me?"

I nodded. "Thank you, I would love to join you."

"Good, we need all the help we can get. They run me ragged over there." She playfully bumped into me with a smile on her face. "Hopefully something gets Clarence back to reality. It's really bothering me. We have Joy to take care of now and if he can't accept his own sister, then how can he expect to be a proper father?"

"I'm sure he sees a difference between the two." I noted. "How is she doing?"

"She still tells me she misses her mother, which I'd like to think makes sense, but truthfully, she was so little when Sally died, there's no way she could remember her. It may be because I tell her stories about her mother all the time, trying to keep her memory alive. That might not be the best way to go about it, but I loved my sister so much, and I want Joy to know her."

"I don't think that's a wrong thing to do." I said.

"But I don't know if she'll ever accept me as her mother, or Clarence as her father. Her father's still alive, but he hasn't even visited once. He's too overwhelmed by everything I think. It was traumatic for him to lose Sally. She was the backbone of the house."

"How long were they married?" I asked.

"Nearly eighteen years." she said with a sigh. "I can't imagine being with someone that long and them dying so suddenly, leaving behind such young children. He was never a very active father because he took so many shifts at the factory to feed everyone and so they had clothes on their backs and shoes on their feet that he missed a lot of time. When Sally died, he just couldn't connect." Minnie shrugged and lay back in the swing, staring at the ceiling of the porch. "I'm not sure Clarence and I will have our own children though, so she's our only chance."

"You're such a kind person, I'm sure that Joy will grow well because of you. My brother is a wonderful man too. He's always been there for me, except for recently of course, but I'm sure he'll make a great father."

"It's been almost a year and we still haven't made all the connections with her." Minnie said, taking a deep breath. "Oh, I shouldn't be worried, I really shouldn't. Either way, I will see you on Wednesday. I'm so excited to bring you, I think you'll love it."

"You're always so excited." I said, hugging her.

What I truly appreciated most of all was Minnie's willingness to be a reasonable Christian and actually listen to what Reverend Perry preached even if he didn't listen to his own words. Minnie came by with a bright smile on her face, her heavy skirt being lifted partially by the wind. I ran outside, Opal following me partially. I sat down on the cart, very aware of the lump on my stomach, forcing me to be shaped oddly and uncomfortably. Minnie climbed back onto the cart and said, "Alright, so today we are going to help prepare and serve some soup. I baked a cake to bring."

"I've been wanting good cake for some time…." I muttered. "Do you think they'd mind if I snuck a piece?"

"It's going to have to be cut beforehand anyways." Minnie laughed. "Is the baby making you hungry then?"

I nodded. "My stomach hasn't been happy with the little one for quite some time and I can't seem to find the right food to fix the cravings."

"You are going to be a wonderful mother."

"I'm glad that you have faith in me. It's nice to hear things like that once in a while."

"I don't doubt your abilities." she said with a smirk, coaxing the horse away from the house and onto the road. "You are always so aware of everything, that baby's going to be in good hands." I touched my swollen belly and left my hand on there, feeling slight movements every once in a while. The fact that there was a child in there still startled me and probably would continue to even after the birth.

When we arrived at the soup kitchen, I was surprised at the fact it was an open brick building with the doors removed. A lot of light poured in through the cloudy windows near the ceiling. There were old tables set up with rough, wooden folding chairs. There were some men wiping them up with wet rags. "Good morning Mrs. Patterson!" A man called from behind the counter. He held a large spoon in his hand as he waved.

"Good morning! I brought some help!" Minnie called with a smile on her face. She still sounded proud of me. Already I felt useful. We walked up to the counter and the man. He had an oddly shaped, comical mustache and a pudgy red face dotted with age. In a way, he didn't look real. "This is my sister-in-law, Virginia Crain."

"It is nice to meet you, Mrs. Crain." he said. "Have you been here before?"

"No, this is my first time." I responded, trying my best to sound as pleasant as humanly possible. I wanted people here to like me. The past location failed miserably, this was my next chance.

"Your help is very welcome here. Minnie knows what to do, just help her out today. Are you with the church too then?"

"Sure." I answered quietly. It was the reverend's words that prompted me, so I might as well give him some credit. I just didn't know if I was considered a member of the church anymore. Minnie and I went into another room, also open to the air. She brought me a large wooden case of vegetables. "We need to wash these up before cutting them, and then we'll add it to the meat that is cooking now in the broth." "Just like home." I said with a smile. We didn't work in silence, instead Minnie told me about anything she could remember, and that was a great deal of memories, events, and what she was looking for in the future including Joy's schooling. She wanted Joy to graduate from school, maybe even go to college. I hadn't thought much about women going to college. The only person I knew who'd gone was Clarence, but of course he met Minnie there so who was I to say? I patiently listened, very interested in her bouncy voice and pervading happiness. I wanted to know how to access it, use it for myself in some way, yet being around her was medicinal. It was wonderful to be away from the house for a little while and the constant clucking of chickens. There was no silence here between Minnie's speaking, the tapping of knives against wood, horse's hooves on the cobblestone, pigeons cooing in the street, and the people milling about in the eating area in the other room.

We filled many cauldrons full of donated vegetables and meat and waited for them to cook. While waiting, we cleaned up some apples and put them in baskets. There was a line of people forming outside, most of which looked tired and ragged. Their hair was unkempt, faces unwashed. For some of them, it was as if the light had been taken from their eyes. Many of them were beggars or homeless convicts who worked odd jobs, others were mothers with too many children who needed their bellies filled. While watching the hungry gather, a woman brought out many loaves of bread and placed them in baskets on the counter. A little thought came into my mind how I could make some bread to bring with me the next time Minnie and I came. It wasn't as if I was going hungry, and I had a roof over my head. It was more than these people could even ask for.

Minnie and I stood in front of the cauldrons with ladles to pour the soup. "Just remember to smile and say hello." she told me. I had to continually remind myself. Each person came up and struggled to make eye contact with me, but once they did, small smiles formed on their face, and they seemed to become a bit lighter when their bowls were filled to the brim and they were carrying away bread. The people sat to-gether, finding fellowship amongst each other. Minnie and I were getting tired being on our feet so much, my ankles were starting to swell and I felt nauseous. I was in good spirits though, and I appreciated that.

We came four times a week, spending half a day to prepare for lunch. I still needed to work on the farm, and keep the house running, so I was still busy. My mind was no longer idle, but I still had time enough to have some leisure. Oliver, who had some experience with carpentry was convinced that he was going to build a cradle for the baby. He was painstakingly attempting to construct it although he didn't have a lot of skill. It wasn't going to be easy, although it was entertaining to watch. He drew a plan of the cradle. He imagined it covered in carvings of hearts and flowers. All the while I made a quilt for the baby. Minnie and I chose the calico cloth to work with, and she bought soft yarn. She would come over and we would sit on the porch, even when it started to get cold. Both of us wanted access to the sun as long as it would stay in the sky. She was a very skilled knitter and created a beautiful soft blanket for the baby while I made a little quilt for the crib.

It was still odd to think that these physical things were evidence that Oliver and I were going to be parents. This child was more than a child or a baby, it was going to grow into a person, who would struggle as the both of us would struggle, but it'd still have support. I knew that we would be good parents. We were open enough to the world that we weren't going to force anything down the child's throat when it came to belief or any other such expectations. We weren't willing to inflict such pain. And we were too aware to be so negligent as not to notice.

Instead when I was very large and heavy and constantly uncomfortable, Oliver and I returned to church. We hadn't gone regularly. I felt ill a majority of the time because of the baby and wasn't willing to risk losing my breakfast all over the church sanctuary, or lose my mind over a headache being prodded by Amos's loud voice. Today, though, I felt like I might as well go before facing the unknown and frankly, dangerous, world of childbirth. The child was so large and active that I was sure it'd be in my arms soon, and I would finally be fully able to relieve myself once again. That was honestly what I looked forward to, and being able to bend over and move easily. I wondered how anyone could stand being obese if they had to survive in such a situation for the rest of their life, carrying around this much weight; even for a few months, the weight bothered me immensely.

I held my breath while we were bouncing along the road. I was worried that any slight movement would cause me to burst, if that was possible. "You look wonderful, Ginny." Oliver said with a sly smile on his face.

"Are you just saying that because I was crying last night about how bad I smelled and how horrible I felt?"

"Yes..." Oliver said, and smiled. "There is nothing to worry about right now. You glow."

"With oil and perspiration." I responded quickly. "God is a cruel, cruel being to put such horrors upon women."

"Horrors?"

"I've been living my entire life, bleeding once a month and then when that ends, I blow up twice my size and have to actually push this thing out. I'd like to see you do that." I hissed.

"I don't think I could." He laughed.

"This is incredibly unpleasant."

"I'm sure it'll be better when it's over." he said, yawning.

While sitting in the pew, I wondered if Amos Perry would ever age, or if he would look like a cross middle-aged man for the rest of his life that was stretched and left out to dry. "And in the celebration of the upcoming arrival of the new Crain baby I would like to speak about the importance of community and family." Him acknowledging us by name startled me and I froze in place. Fear creeped through me and the nausea returned with a vengeance. "It is central to our humanity to grow, and watch others grow, to nurture others, especially our own. It is a joy to know that we are bringing a life into this church, into a future with hope, and purpose. Psalm 127 says: Behold, children are a heritage from the Lord, the fruit of the womb a reward. Like arrows in the hand of a warrior are the children of one's youth. Blessed is the man who fills his quiver with them. He shall not be put to shame when he speaks with his enemies at the gate. Matthew says: You are the salt of the earth, but if salt has lost its taste, how shall its saltiness be restored? It is no longer good for anything except to be thrown out and trampled under people's feet. You are the light of the world. A city set on a hill cannot be hidden. Nor do people light a lamp, and put it under a basket, but on a stand, and it gives light to all in the house. In the same way, let your light shine before others, so that they may see your good work and give glory to your Father who is in heaven." His voice echoed throughout the wooden halls of the church.

"It is the responsibility of all of us to assist this child in growing up in a world that is worth living in, or a world that is worth being changed. Rather, speaking the truth in love, we are to grow up in every way into him who is the head, into Christ, from whom the whole body joined and held together by every joint which it is equipped, when each part is working properly moves the body grow so that it builds itself up in love. It is with this message I must tell you, the world is changing. We see it. We are facing a head on collision with new forces trying to uproot all that is good and righteous in this world. Youth these days are denying their elders moral authority, they are beginning to show that they are nothing more than the fruit of social disorder and disintegration. Our society is shattering right before our very eyes. Our young are left adrift by the failures of society. Our families are supposed to be the bulwark of our youth. We are not allowed to be indulgent or permissive. We must teach them self-control, we must teach them to be moral. We must be able to survive this change with our families intact. We must provide firm doctrine not idealism could provide our children with stable lives."

Chapter Seventeen

And into the strange, uncomfortable world that was mother-hood, and the fear that came with the unknown, Oliver and I quickly learned how to adjust. My family was present in my house as soon as labor began. I was fed by Miriam's cooking. Minnie was with me, holding my hand, trying to help me along with the pain, and I realized that I didn't know true physical pain until this moment. It was an ultimatum of sorts, that everything in my life would change after this moment. I only hoped everyone got out of the situation alive. Oliver was beside me, much against my mother's wishes, thinking that there shouldn't be any men nearby during this process. I complained and cried enough, though, and for once, I got what I wanted.

The view in the bedroom changed in this setting. There were lamps and candles set up everywhere to try to illuminate properly once evening set. There was a glare over my eyes during the later stages of labor, making the world fuzzy, possibly from the candlelight intermingling with a scrunched face and tears. Minnie patted my forehead with a cold cloth and she coached me along. Her late sister, whom I had become incredibly familiar without ever having met the lady, was a midwife, and her brother was a doctor. Although she had no experience doing this alone, she assisted her sister on enough occasions that I hoped I would be safe, and so would the baby. She was the only one here I could trust to pull me through this situation.

My mother sat in the living room, her hands clasped tight together, praying. She was in sight of me. There was such strain on her face, I only wished I knew the words she was saying to God. At the moment, I was crying to God to make this go speedily and well, and to remove some of the pain. Minnie said, "I see it! I see the baby's head! You're doing so well, Ginny, so well!" I let out a wail, and felt no relief. "Keep going on, Ginny, come on!"

"That's it," Oliver said, grasping my hand tighter. I screeched again, feeling the pressure mixed with a slight bit of relief.

"There we go." Minnie said quietly, and she held up the screaming, red child dripping wet with fluid. "You have a daughter!"

I tried to see properly. Soon she whisked the baby away after Oliver cut the cord so she could wash her. I lay back in bed, staring at the ceiling, heart pounding, feeling exhausted. Oliver patted my shoulder and he said, "Did you see her? Did you see how healthy she looked?"

I nodded. "I want to hold her! I want to hold her!" Minnie returned, the baby wrapped up in the blanket she had knitted. I smiled and took a hold of the child. She rested in my arms just as she was supposed to, cradled and comfortable. She stopped crying and she began to look around the world. "Welcome to the world, Miss Sally Crain."

Minnie smiled and a tear fell down her cheek. "Welcome back to the world,"

Oliver kissed my cheek as my parents came in to see the baby. Their faces were full of joy, a joy I hadn't seen in a long time. They were very happy to hold her, and I was given praise for having become a mother. For having been able to prove that we were what we were supposed to be, a functioning married couple, since that's what married people do, they have children.

As I watched my mother hold Sally, I wondered what kind of world I brought her into, whether or not it was a world I wanted her to witness, to be a part of. I knew she would never be sheltered enough not to suffer, and that was not the best path to follow regardless. As Perry said, the world was falling to pieces around us. It would probably continue to do so since it's been doing so since the beginning of time. Would she in fact have the ability to be happy, to face everything with courage? To be brave? Could that be taught?

I wanted her to be a person. I was blessed with my situation to be seen as a living being with opinions and purpose. Not all were so lucky, and those that were, needed to be grateful. Soon after I was cleaned up, I fell into a deep sleep with Oliver at my side. Sally woke me near five that morning with her chirping cries. Before she began her wailing, I moved my arm out of my linen nightgown, and she latched onto me. She was hungry. She stared ahead as she nursed until her eyes closed. She continued to suckle until she was fast asleep. I lay her back on the bed beside Oliver who was curled up facing my side of the bed. I stood up for a moment to stretch. My body was sore, and my insides felt completely different now that she was no longer inside me. Sally looked so small, so fragile, and yet when she cried, she sounded so alive and so powerful.

I stepped out of the bedroom, as silently as I could manage. Leaving the door open, I saw Minnie was still asleep in the living room. My stomach cramped and nausea rushed through me. I placed my hand on my deflated tummy and held by breath, hoping for it to pass. My body was exhausted, having fought to survive through birth this far, but there was so much discomfort I had to move around. Tingling flew through my hands and legs, and I paced a bit before going back to bed. Being near Oliver and Sally put me at ease. I touched her soft, tiny little hands. She moved idly in her sleep. Curling up near her, I fell asleep.

Morning came with the smell of toast being made over the fire burning stove. It couldn't have been more than an hour and a half after I last laid down. Oliver yawned beside me. I smiled at him and said, "Look what we did, what we have." He smiled as well and touched Sally's cheek.

"She's perfect." Oliver said. "You did wonderful."

"I'm so tired." I said with a laugh. "It doesn't feel real, that we have her... we did it, Oliver, we did it."

The following week, I felt well enough to take Sally to church for the first and only time. I was painfully aware of how small she was, how vulnerable. How something so small could scream and cry so loudly, I didn't know, but she was very vocal and she let me know when she was hungry or wanted something, and by God if she was ever tired and didn't have the proper situation to sleep in, I'd get a mouthful of complaints. Even as we were on the way to the church, she was cooing against my breast. I held her protectively as if to shelter her from the eyes.

Since Sally had come along Oliver felt much more comfortable in the world, like he had a place and his feet were on the ground. It was a special thing to see, that a person I loved was feeling good, and was doing well too. He wasn't even wearing my satin nightgown underneath of his shirt, much to my relief. There was nothing to be afraid of today.

We were greeting by a multitude of people wanting to see and hold the baby. There were people smiling and giggling.

It was like nothing bad ever happened, just because we were holding a new person in our arms and I had spent nine months carrying her around, and a day and a half trying to bring her into the world. I almost forgot about all the pain involved in this despite how imprinting it should have been. Instead we became new as well.

Sitting in the pew, I prayed to God that Sally would stay quiet during the next hour. The very idea of that was almost impossible, but I could hope nonetheless. Amos smiled when he saw us and stood at the pulpit. "It is a great day when we can see the miracle of what God has given us, love and life. It is a great day when the sun is shining and we are comfortable and under the shelter of his protection. We all have the ability to reach for perfection, to reach for the goals God has placed in front of us, outlined by his words. Peter states: so put away all malice and all deceit and hypocrisy and envy and all slander. Like newborn infants, long for the pure spiritual milk, that by it you may grow up into salvation if indeed you have tasted the Lord is good. As you come to him, a living stone rejected by men but in the sight of God chosen and precious, you yourselves like living stones are being built up as a spiritual house. Like little Sally here, new to the world, there is no evil within her. There is nothing of hate, or anger. There is only pure love and pure needs and nothing more, yet a blank slate that can be taught and molded, to grow into what is a beloved creation of God."

Perry's expectations of Sally weighed on my mind, dangling above my face as something that must be achieved. It was my duty to create what she needed to be, as if she had no life of her own. No thoughts of her own. At the moment that was true, she just seemed to be a drooling, defecating, crying blob of adorable flesh. Thankfully, though, Sally was quiet, very comfortable to stay on my lap with her head buried in between my arm and breast. She listened quite intently to Amos during the entire sermon. I was concerned that she could understand his words, or even believe what he was saying. I wanted her to remain innocent, not corrupt with fear as Amos corrupted me, as my mother corrupted me. In that pew, surrounded by my family, I told myself that I would never take a switch to my daughter to force her to sit up straight or conform. She had too much to worry about already. She had all these expectations and the entire world ahead of her.

And yet I was still here, in this building. I was already made to conform. I might as well make the most of it. As the organ played the processional tune and we lined up to exit the sanctuary one arm held Sally against my body and the other grasped Oliver's hand. Oliver squeezed my hand and a smile crossed my face. Clarence stood behind me, eyes staring down on me with concern. If looks could kill, our hands would have melted off. I kissed Sally's forehead and she kissed me back. So much joy was on her face. She was gorgeous. Perfect. Her little curls bounced as we moved to the door. I moved to the side, away from Reverend Perry, others could shake his hand, give him their weekly update on their life. I wasn't interested. After thinking I was safe, Mother approached me. My automatic motion was to stand up straighter than before. "Virginia, I let the ladies know that you would be joining the group today."

I sighed and shook my head. "I should be getting home with Sally…"

Before I had time to finish speaking, Mother interjected, "I promised that they would be able to meet my granddaughter."

"Alright Mother." I responded. She still had control over me. I felt like she physically managed to twist my soul into a writhing mess being dragged where it would rather not be dragged.

When the long hand of the clock hit the 8- I went into the Blue Room and took a seat near the door with Sally. Women poured in soon after, most of them came over, ignoring my presence, kissed Sally and showered her with compliments. Mother sat right beside me. Usually she never sat this near the door. She liked the back, inconspicuous enough that it would keep her 'humble'. The women sat down on time, eyes fixed on the baby like she was some sort of lump of gold. "Welcome back, Virginia, welcome back." Mrs. Baker said smoothly. I didn't trust her. I didn't trust anyone in this room.

"This is my granddaughter, Sally." Mother said.

"Beautiful child, such a future ahead of her." Miss Maggie said with pride, beaming with happiness.

"It's a big responsibility, Virginia. You know that this life is up to you, to determine whether or not she will be able to go to heaven or hell." Mrs. Baker said.

I wanted to laugh. It took a matter of two minutes before hell was mentioned. Two minutes. All I wanted was some peace. "She's going to be fine under my care." I said carefully. "She's a good girl."

"Under the right circumstances, she will be." Mrs. Baker said.

"And what does that mean?" I added protectively, holding tightly onto Sally. She melted into me like she could sense this as well.

Another woman took in a deep breath and said, "If no one else will say it, I might as well, she came from bad seed. Your daughter came from bad seed."

"Is that why I'm here? Is that what this is about?" I cried.

Mother took in a deep breath. "I speak for all the women when I say that you need to make decisions, decisions that will determine important outcomes for your daughter."

"Please, explain." I said with heat and anger in my voice.

"Because your husband is an abomination." Mother said. "A homosexual. He's detestable to God."

I chuckled and shook my head. "You're mad. Mad." I stood up, adjusting Sally. My eyes fell on Miss Maggie, pleadingly. Her eyes watered and she looked down to her feet, more deflated than I'd ever seen her before, but she wasn't moving. She wasn't going to save me. I was alone.

"You need to leave him, Virginia." Mrs. Baker said.

"You all are cruel," I said. "You don't listen to God; you make a mockery of him."

Almost in tears I stepped out of the Blue Room and slammed the door, walking quickly out to the cart. It was empty, Oliver was nowhere to be found. I climbed in and crumbled up, crying. Sally started to cry too. My body was shaking with the purest of anger. "Oliver!" I cried. "Oliver!"

He emerged from a corn field, put his hat on his head and jumped in, getting the horse in motion onto the road. "What happened?"

"Just go... just go..." I muttered. "Please..."

Chapter Eighteen

After ten months of watching my daughter grow, I adjusted back to a regular schedule of life, all was well. Oliver and I were never better together. We didn't worry about the people at church. We didn't worry about my family. There was no fear, and there was no confusion. I could consider myself to be happy. I woke one morning, lying beside Oliver. I placed my head on his shoulder and watched as he breathed. I kissed his ear until he chuckled and woke, turning towards me. A smile crossed his face and he kissed my nose. I stretched, happy that Sally had slept through the night. "Do you want me to check on her?" Oliver asked, yawning heavily. I simply nodded and buried my head in the pillow again. Oliver returned and placed the baby next to me. She began to pull on my hair, indicating that she was being impatient, and was hungry. I sat up slowly and nursed her.

"George mailed me saying they will be visiting in three days. They are bringing the car by."

"Them and that car." I said. "It looks like it's more trouble than it's worth."

"That's what Clara says about children." Oliver replied, placing his hand on Sally's soft golden hair.

"I suppose that's why they have been avoiding having children." I responded. "Not exactly sure how they'd avoid it, they just… show up." Oliver smiled a bit and lay back down, staring at the ceiling. Sally pulled at my necklace that was hanging from my neck. "And are you going to be joining us?"

"It'll be Saturday."

"Oh, I'm getting my days all mixed up." I said, kissing Sally's forehead. I picked her up and laid her on the bed. She sat up and began to babble away. "I really want to know what is going on in her mind."

"Only God knows." Oliver responded.

I dressed well for our excursion out into the open, bringing a shawl Minnie just completed for me to keep warm with the frigid wind that had picked up today. Sally walked about unevenly on the ground, and she always talked. I explained to her what we were going to do, ride in an automobile. She'd never been in one before, only had she seen a few on the road back and forth from church. Her world was a small one, but it was one she was comfortable with and one she was safe in.

The automobile puttered over and George parked it. Clara ran out and when she saw Sally and she kissed the girl's cheek and said, "Look how wonderful you are! Oh and you are getting so big so quickly! You were so little last time I saw you!" Then she hugged me. "And look how well you are! Oh Oliver where are you?" she called into the house.

"I'll be there in just a moment!" Oliver replied.

"Come on! Hurry up!" I answered. "We don't have all day!"

"Yes, we do!" he responded. He stepped out looking all dapper, wearing his nice new felt hat. I smiled from ear to ear.

"Now that's a handsome young man," Clara said. She patted his shoulder and we went to the car. Sally walked beside slowly, and I held her hand. She was learning to get her legs moving how she wanted them too, but most of the time she just ran into the walls and furniture, like she didn't have the ability to stop. "Are you ready to go into town?" Clara asked, eyeing Sally. Sally nodded in response.

"Looks like we are." I added. We pulled into the road and down past the fields. Sally watched intently, a smile on her face. She put her hands in the air to feel it as we sped through. The wind was truly very invigorating.

"Oh look how beautiful her curls are and she's just so cute." Clara said to George, patting his arm.

"I'm driving." he said.

"Oh, but just a peak before she stops being so interested, George!" Clara prodded.

There was a moment when I saw both of their faces peering at Sally, Oliver and I. There was a smile on Clara's lipstick lined lips and her mascaraed lashes. She held onto the feathered hat and waved to Sally with the other hand. George had a calm smile past his shy exterior. I noticed that the tweed he wore was frayed.

And that's all I know. In a moment the automobile became a pile of twisted metal, and my mind was not present to witness it. In a moment I felt so light, airy, that I could be floating in pure air. It was sweet and yet harsh, the wind hitting me with such force that I felt like my flesh would be ripped from my bones. And then I realized that I didn't have a body. There was nothing around me but blackness, and the sensation that I was in a physical place. There was a bounciness to this place, that I was being pushed from every direction. My feet, if I had feet, were not planted on any ground.

I tried to move throughout the space, to find a direction to go in, to find what was next. There was no fear in me, nothing but a sense of ease and peace. It was pervasive and beautiful even.

That feeling only lasted for but a little while longer, until I felt such pressure on me, driving me down quickly into the ground. I was shoved back onto the earth. When I opened my eyes, I was in bed, hardly able to breathe. Every bit of my body was in pain, crying out for relief. It was so sudden, even unwelcome. My head was pounding with the same pressure. I kept my eyes open, trying to adjust to the blurry vision. Everything looked strange, as if this was only a replica of my room, yet I could not tell any discernable difference. My mind was playing tricks on me. A hand touched mine, and I turned my head to see Oliver looking at me. He smiled a bit, sadly, weakly. He looked as if he was lying there for no purpose, but then I realized that there was a thick bandage across his middle, and it was soaked with blood. I saw the baby crib to the side, but couldn't see in it.

With all my energy I knew that I wanted to see Sally. She had to be alright. I couldn't live if she didn't make it. She was everything to me. Fear invaded me quickly, going through my veins. I tried to stand up, my arms were loose and weak. When my bare feet reached the ground, even the floor felt foreign. I stood up a bit, but then realized I wasn't going to be standing any longer. I fell straight down to the wooden ground, face smacking into the floor. All the breath was pushed out of me, and then I lay there, trying to understand what I felt. I realized I wasn't breathing anymore. I wasn't moving either. Yet I was aware of everything around me. Feet came rushing towards the room and I was lifted off the ground. I opened my eyes again and saw George. There was sadness and pity washing his face. "I am glad you are both awake." he said.

"What happened…?" I breathed, my voice cracking. It sounded different.

He placed me back in the bed and put the quilt on top of me. "You need to stay in this bed for now, Ginny. You aren't well." He sat down at the foot of the bed. "We were in an automobile accident. The back of the automobile was hit by another automobile when we went on the road." He took in a deep breath and looked to Oliver. "You were hit very hard in the head, Ginny."

I touched my head and felt a soft spot that was coated in blood. It was clotted and black. I always remembered blood being a dark red. There was blood on the pillow. Shocked I felt like I was frozen. Clara stepped in. "Let me change that...." she muttered, taking the pillow. "We will make sure you all three get better."

"Sally?" I asked.

"She's right over there. She's alright."

I nodded, relieved, and lay my head back on the pillow. My mind wouldn't stay in my body hardly, and I continued to return to the light feeling, only to be rushed back into my body every few minutes. Soon, though, I felt so stiff. I couldn't move my head, but could only stare ahead. Clara poured water down my throat, but it didn't satiate the thirst that was pounding through my body and down into my stomach. Oliver was coughing up blood and was writhing in pain. I wished I could comfort him, I wished I could move and hold him, but no matter what I thought, or wished to do, I couldn't. My mind couldn't even focus enough to hardly think. I just was.

While I was still frozen in this hell, I woke once, and Oliver wasn't beside me. The bed was made and there was not even an indent in the pillow. There was some talking in the parlor. Everyone walked out of the front door, which I could see from the open door and they closed it behind them. I heard the sound of the cart and the clicks of the horses as they moved out from the house. Opal jumped up next to me and sniffed the bed. She looked at me curiously and placed her paw on my head before lying down next to me, and she began to cry. I'd never heard a cat cry in a way that sounded like grief. I forced my arm to move just slightly and placed it on the soft cat's back. She began to purr and rubbed her head against mine.

A smile crossed my face just slightly, something resembling comfort and I moved my hand just slightly to pet her. Her paw rested on my cheek, and she began to knead just a little bit.

At some point in the evening, everyone returned. Clara and George went into the kitchen and Oliver walked in. He sat down beside me. "You are looking very well." I said with a smile.

He nodded and said, "I'm feeling well. I'm better." He took in a deep breath and touched my hand. "Come on, stand up." he pressed. "Let's see if you can."

I moved my legs to the side of the bed, amazed that I could move at all. He held onto my hand and kept good eye contact. I stood up, feeling extremely heavy. I smiled a bit and said, "I'm standing."

"You are." A smile broke across his face. I took a few more steps, feeling my heart race forward like it'd jump out of my chest. I walked over to the cradle and saw Sally lying there. She was pale, motionless, I touched her skin and it was cold. I screamed in despair, and Oliver stepped back, shocked, and sat down on the edge of the bed.

George ran back and put his hands on my shoulders. "What is it Virginia?"

"She's... she's dead!" I cried, holding my hand up to my mouth. Tears flowed down my cheeks and I collapsed on the floor, feeling weak again. George struggled to assist me to stand again and he sighed.

"No, no, Virginia, your daughter is fine. You need to rest. You need to lie back down."

"You're lying!" I said. "Why are you lying to me?"

"No, dear. I'm not lying to you. I promise." He picked the child up and her head was lying to the side, her eyes were closed. I didn't see any breath coming from her. The limpness of her body was startling, like she'd melt right in his arms. My beautiful baby was dead and no one saw it. He held her and touched her hair before taking her out into the parlor. I lay down on the bed and buried my head in the pillow and sobbed. Oliver stayed near me, touching my back, doing everything he could to comfort me. "My baby is dead... how could she be dead? How could God take her away from me like that?"

"Shh... Virginia, you need to rest." Oliver said, touching my cheek. "You don't want to make your wounds worse."

"Why aren't you angry? God took our baby away!" I cried.

"I can't argue with God." Oliver said, sitting against the bedframe. He wrapped his arms around me tightly. "And neither can you."

That evening there was a knock on the door frame. Clara held a tray with food on it and she stepped in. I sat up a bit and stared at the well-cooked food on the tray, eggs, bread and butter. There was no hunger in my belly, just what felt like a partially empty, contorted mess. "Thank you," I said to Clara who nodded and sat beside me. Oliver was fast asleep, with his head comfortably cradled on a feather pillow. I bit into the buttered bread, and within a moment, it turned to dust in my mouth, absorbing any remaining moisture. My mouth suddenly turned dry and I choked and spit it out. On the tray there was a dark grey dust. I drank down the water and tried to remove it from my mouth. No amount of water would fix the problem. "What is wrong with it?" Clara asked, startled.

"Look, it's ash!" I cried, pointing at it.

"I don't see it." Clara said, concern pasting her face. "It's just bread, Ginny."

"I'm not eating anymore of it." I said, putting my hands up.

"You need to eat something, Virginia. You'll get even sicker if you don't."

"I'm not eating ashes." I stated strongly.

"Alright, we'll try again later…" Clara sighed, looking deflated. She closed the door behind her and I turned to Oliver. I placed my hand on his shirt. He felt cold through it the linen cloth. I pulled the blanket up to his chest. He turned towards me and kissed my cheek. His eyes were serene, soft, familiar.

"I'm so confused, Oliver." I said, trying to sit up.

"You will be for some time, Ginny."

"Do you know what is wrong with me?" I asked.

"You were hurt very badly in the automobile accident." he responded, his voice floating easily through air. "You were struck in the head."

"Did you see it happen?" I asked. He nodded. "Am I alive?"

"You're here, aren't you?" he answered.

"The food though… I couldn't eat it. And what happened to Sally?" I paused, trying to wrap my mind around everything. "It's all their fault! Clara and George! They weren't paying attention to the raod!" I cried. "They killed my baby!" I felt acid leak through my body, making me shake with anger and frustration, but I did not have the adrenaline or ability leap out of bed and release it.

"Virginia…" Oliver said soothingly. "You need to be calm. You're going to hurt yourself if you're not."

"Why? Why do I need to be calm? Nothing is making sense! Nothing… nothing… nothing…" I buried my head in my hands and felt as if I was melting. My body was burning hot, and I could smell myself. I fell out of bed and ripped off my stockings and lay on the cold wood, hoping to get relief. I needed to wash up. The stench coming from my body only grew. I crawled to the washbasin and grabbed the bar of soap. I pulled myself to sit on the chair and started washing. My own skin looked utterly pale, as if it'd been removed from the sun for a great deal of time, or as if it'd never seen the sun at all. I sprayed my body with toilet water and stared in the mirror. My hair was matted and my eyes were sunken. I took the comb and tried to smooth my hair out. It seemed slightly longer, and it felt very dry like straw.

Something was wrong past a bad injury.

Chapter Nineteen

I was dead. I had to be dead, or cursed. Something. I was still walking this earth, locked in the body of a dead woman, my own body. I was still aware, seeing, feeling, experiencing. Those around me couldn't see it, but I could. I tried to get clean, to remove the smell of my own body rotting, but all it did was pull flesh off in clumps. It peeled off like jelly, and I gathered it together in an old waste basket and wrapped the wounds with linen and continually sprayed myself with the toilet water to cover up the smell of death with that of flowers. My body still felt weak, but it was eating itself up. Trying to get a breath of fresh air, I sat outside on the rocking chair watching as the world was still turning, but I could only imagine why I was returned here to watch it from this body. There must have been a purpose, but whatever it was, it was foreign.

I was never alone, though. Clara or George, or Minnie were always here, especially Minnie though. She would flit around the house, carrying Sally's corpse just as Clara and George still did. She'd sing and cook things that I couldn't eat. With Minnie, nothing weighed on her. Nothing at all, even such a desperate situation. I felt like I needed to be silent, like I was carrying some secret that God didn't want released. My heart was heavy with the passing of my daughter, although light that I still had Oliver. He was gone during the day at work still, and was with me at night. Nothing, though, could fix the fact that I had a similarly decaying body lying in the cradle at night. At times I watched over here, seeing her lie there motionless, without breath. She looked at peace, yet I could see that she had become incredibly bloated with gases. Pieces of her skin stretched so tight that it looked translucent. Her face was almost unrecognizable. Bugs started to crawl around her eyes and mouth, eating away at the soft flesh. I didn't dare touch her. I was afraid to feel what I'd become soon. The moonlight landed on her white face and kissed her like she was an angel. I imagined that she was up in heaven, probably in the care of Minnie's Sally. She at least had a care-giver to go to, but I was angry that she left me alone. She was my hope for a future, and she left me. God took her from me.

While I was outside, I prayed to God for answers. I didn't know where else to turn. I felt cursed, and I wanted to know why. What had I done to be placed in this situation? Was I truly as evil as my parents believed? Did God shape me to become their worst fear? Or mine? At times, though, I felt at ease though, while my head was bowed and I was speaking freely to what was far more than just the sky and the air. It felt like God was doing his best to comfort me. I kept my eyes closed, focusing on the world around me, expecting to feel the answer come to me. Once when I was a child, I heard the voice of God, and I believed it was a gift never to be experienced again.

I remembered it so clearly that it could have happened just a few days prior. I was in the family garden, gathering up produce, mainly peas and string beans. I had a large basket filled when I became tired and sat under the large maple tree to escape the hot beams of sun. I broke open a few pods and ate the sweet peas inside, discarding the shells. Then the heard my name come from above, separate than that of my parents, invading me throughout, and surrounding me. Everything stopped. The birds in the air, the chickens near the coop. Nothing moved, nothing dared. I stood up, fear and awe simultaneously filling me. I ran inside and hid, expecting for the voice to continue. It was only my name though, but I knew where it came from.

Now though, I opened my eyes and saw the answer God wanted me to see. One of the horses stood at the edge of the pasture, looking straight to me. It was skeletal, pale, her eyes were completely black holes. Startled, I held onto the handles of the rocking chair and watched as it began to run through the pasture which was also completely dead. There was no green, only brown and gold grass. The other horses were lying on the ground, bloated and rotting, being scavenged by ravens and vultures which were fighting each other away.

Wishing to no longer see the horror before me, I shuffled my way back inside and into the parlor. I closed my eyes again, hoping that the world would return to normal. I focused on every other sound, that of the cats mewing and walking about, Minnie's feet on the wooden floor in the kitchen. When I opened my eyes and looked out the door, all was returned to normal. There were no dead horses, and the pines were still green. "Am I mad?" I asked, my voice feeling like it left my body.

Minnie turned to me. She knelt next to me, taking my hands in hers. "Are you mad? Why do you say that?"

"I'm dead." I said. "But you see me, and I'm still here."

She took in a deep breath and nodded. "My dear, you aren't dead."

"I'm falling to pieces. Please believe me…"

"Perhaps it would be nice if you saw a physician to see if there isn't anything he can do to make you feel better." Minnie said, putting her hand on my hair. "I will have Clarence arrange an appointment. A physician visited while you were still on bedrest, but you didn't have these symptoms then."

"He will only tell us all that I'm mad." I muttered.

"And if that's the truth?" she asked, looking me in the eye.

"I don't want it to be true…" I cried. "I only wish that we were never in that automobile!"

"I do too, Virginia. Please, be patient. You will be well again. I promise, and I'll be there until that happens."

The only hope I truly had for being well again, was to reach that dark place where I floated, where I could believe that I wouldn't return to this body, to actually die. Yet if that was where I was damned to be, on this earth, to watch it fall to pieces, I didn't know what to do. There was nothing I really could do except be a witness to it. There was something to say for fate, for God's hands to be involved in my life. Before, there'd never been a presence of something directing me each step, and even now, I felt as if there was some kind of free will, but the biggest decisions, or placements such as my current experience, were made by God, and that caused me to feel small, helpless, and weak. In that same thought though, it made me feel partially safe. Father always used to say that God would never place on us what he thought we couldn't handle, even if that was death. If he trusted me this much, I must be something in his eyes. There must be some significance to my life, and yet all this time, I'd never seen it. I considered myself existent, not alive, not using my life for anything but eating, sleeping, washing, and now even what could be evidence of my life was gone, my Sally, but I was seeing things that no one else was seeing. The world was painted differently. It didn't feel like the truth though, it felt like God was playing tricks on me. I didn't know what to believe.

Everything that once was safe and understandable, was now seen through the eyes of reality. There was death and famine, and destruction coming upon us, just as Perry believed. The world was going to fall into chaos. There was a floating darkness in the air, twisting around trees, flowing through the wind and water. There was light and colors dancing around different people. Minnie looked like light was within her. Clara looked like there was cynicism in her. George looked guilt ridden and shy. Sally, who was still lying in the cradle, deflated and ridden with bugs, had no light about her because she wasn't there. She was somewhere in heaven, safe from all of this. She would never see what I was seeing, and that could be considered a relief. She was safe. That was my consolation, my only consolation.

I couldn't stand seeing her decomposing body though. The stench that surrounded her was hellish. Sally didn't deserve for the world to watch her turn to dust. I went outside to the barn. The strong scent of the horse stalls hit me. Light flowed through the holes in the ceiling Oliver had yet to patch up. The spade lay on the ground beside the feed bins. I picked it up, and went to an empty space next to the chicken coop. I stepped on the space, breaking into the soft ground. It fell apart beneath the weight, and piled it beside the burgeoning grave. I wanted to make it deep for my baby, so she wouldn't be stepped on so close to the surface. I thought of the flowers I could plant above her, so she had a marker, something beautiful and fragrant. I jumped into the grave now, it was up to my chest. In a way, I thought I could just lay down in it with her. I wanted to stay with my baby forever, but I couldn't leave Oliver behind.

"Ginny?" Minnie's voice rang through the air.

"I'm over here!" I called from the back of the house. She walked along the wrap around porch, and put her hand up to her head to shield her eyes from the sun.

"What are you doing?"

"I need a place to bury her!"

"Who?"

"Sally!" I said.

She ran over, holding her dress up and she seized the spade from me. "Get out of there, Ginny, come on." she snapped. "Stop, now. No, you can't do that, Ginny. She doesn't need a grave." She reached for me and I climbed out of the hole and onto the grassy ground. "We need to fill it back in, Ginny."

"She needs a place to go…" I muttered.

"No, she doesn't." Minnie said sternly. "Come on, help me fill it back in."

Clarence arranged for me to see a physician in the city. He had the audacity to come to retrieve Minnie and I in an automobile. I wrapped myself up and sat in the back. I didn't feel worried though, if I was to get hit again, possibly this time I would actually die. This time I could join Sally, and be safe. Yet that would mean that I would leave Oliver behind, and he would sleep alone at night, yet what was sleeping beside a dead woman anyways? He didn't deserve that.

I closed my eyes, feeling myself move through space while sitting in the back of the automobile. Wind whistled past us and the ground hummed beneath us. There was a sense that I could be lifted off the ground at any moment, and I waited and prayed for that to occur. Minnie was beside me, and she patiently placed her hand on mine, to ground me. "We are almost there, Ginny."

I opened my eyes and focused on all the tall buildings; connecting to one another, made of brick, scarring and flattening the ground. It was the opposite of art, opposite of all God had intended, and yet it was here. People were walking about, many looked dead, just like me. Their eyes were hollow, their bones were prominent, they looked deflated of all life. There was hardly any light surrounding them, like a dying candle being snuffed out. There was a pervasive sadness covering these people, while a few actually looked very much alive, like all the light in the world was directed much toward them. There was such a disparity between the two. People like Minnie, who exuded liveliness amongst all this pain seemed so unique and beautiful. Their light looked like the light that went through a diamond: reflecting off of numerous surfaces, sparkling and alive. But there was also a floating dark green mist, going towards people, constricting them, one to the other. It felt like sickness in the form of seaweed, but light enough it could travel through air.

Clarence opened the door for us and assisted me in walking forward. My legs were shaky, they didn't have any strength left in them. His arm was locked with mine. There was some compassion in his eyes, I was thankful for that. Yet, it felt artificial. The doctor's office had a large porcelain sign above it that just said 'Doctor' and on the door it listed a Dr. Michael Goldman written on a plaque. Minnie opened the door and a small bell rang. The office smelled very sweet, and there was a jar of caramels on the counter. A secretary was there, and she looked up to us with a bright smile. Clarence whispered to her that Virginia Crain had an appointment before we sat down. The woman across from me was heavily pregnant. She looked alive. But I could see the baby curled up in her belly. It turned to look at me, it's eyes painfully innocent. It reminded me of Sally. Sally was in my belly at one point, innocent, and alive. I touched my deflated belly, wishing she was still there, so I could keep her safe.

I noticed that there was another light hanging above the mother, in the shape of someone looking down upon her, its arm draped on her shoulder. Someone missed her, but the shape didn't betray any details, that's all it was, a shape created from light. The doctor stepped out from a door beside the secretary. He was a large man with wire glasses sitting on his nose. I took a hold of Minnie; I didn't want to go alone. When he welcomed me to follow him, Minnie and I stepped through the threshold and into an examination room. There was a large clouded window that let in a lot of light in before the table bed where I sat, my feet dangling above the tile floor. Dr. Goldman smiled and said, "It is nice to meet you Mrs. Crain. Your brother came and told me that since your automobile wreck you have been suffering from some head injuries." I nodded. "Would you mind telling me what you are having difficulty with?"

"They think I'm mad…" I said quietly.

Minnie became tense beside me, sitting up straighter, her shoulders rounding out. She kept her hands clamped together. "In what ways, Mrs. Crain?"

"I feel as though I am dead." I responded quietly. "My body is dead. And I'm seeing strange things…"

His face contorted a bit. I feared he didn't believe me. There was no reason for him to believe me. He said, "Well, first I'm going to see how your head fared in that wreck." He moved my hair aside and touched the sensitive injuries on my head. He took a light and told me to follow it, but as he said that, I peered into his eyes and saw a green glimmering light within him. As kind as he seemed, something too was plaguing him. It started to pour out of his eyes in a thick matted goo and onto the floor. "Mrs. Crain, I need you to focus now." he said. He didn't respond to the mess coming out of his eyes and gathering on the floor. Just as soon as it hit the tile it was absorbed into the space between the tiles.

He sighed and sat down and asked, "Could you tell me more about what you see?"

I mentioned the goo that came from his eyes, what I saw near the woman in the waiting room, and the horses in the pasture, and that I was sure my own daughter was dead. He looked over to Minnie, "Do you think you could bring your husband in, Mrs. Patterson?"

The light that was all around Minnie, seemed to dim a bit as she stepped out to retrieve Clarence. He came in quickly and almost slammed the door behind him, but startled by his own actions, slowed it so it closed normally with a click. Clarence didn't sit, he just stood beside Minnie and kept a hand on her shoulder. Dr. Goldman took in a deep breath before he said, "I fear that the head injury has caused some detrimental damage to your sister's brain, and greatly, her mind. I believe that you need to make some important decisions, whether you'd be willing to confine her to your home or hers and have her supervised or to place her in a mental hospital, an asylum. Although I don't believe she is currently dangerous, this delusion and madness could grow into hysteria."

Clarence froze, his body growing stiff and he nodded. "I understand," he began. "We have the ability to keep her at her home."

Dr. Goldman nodded. "What's happened here is very curious, I would like to see her in a few weeks, to see if anything has changed, but she should be confined to home. Any more stress on her mind may cause the effects to get worse."

"Of course." Clarence put his arm around me and started to lead me out. The doctor was extremely unhelpful. He was supposed to make me feel better, wasn't he? Locking me up wasn't going to do anyone any good. Clarence and Minnie were silent as we returned to the house. I closed my eyes again, partially because I just didn't want to see anything else I wasn't supposed to see. Yet as I did so, I continued to smell myself. I could feel something crawling beneath my skin, but with every bit of strength and concentration in my mind and body not to respond to the stimuli while Minnie and Clarence were near.

Clarence stepped out and looked at me through the window of his new automobile. "You know what this means now, Virginia?"

"Yes, but I don't agree." I said.

"You don't need to agree…" Clarence sighed, heat coming through his voice. He opened the door. "Someone will be here all the time to make sure you're taken care of."

"You don't understand…" I mumbled.

"No, I don't." he said as Minnie and I stepped out. "You are clearly unfit right now to take care of yourself and your daughter."

"Why does there need to be someone here all the time?" I asked.

"I just told you. Now go inside." He pointed to the door and spoke very sternly. It was as if I was walking to my death, going up those steps to the house. I was painfully aware as they squeaked beneath my feet and how the door clicked shut. I stepped up to the cradle where Minnie leaned over Sally. Clara left once they arrived. Minnie touched her cheek and the baby didn't respond. She seemed to stall in decomposition.

The crawling sensation didn't cease; only did it grow over the next few moments. "I will go make some dinner." Minnie said quietly. I sat down at the vanity and opened the drawer to find Oliver's knife. He was asleep behind me. He seemed very happy to lounge in bed once returning home from work.

He said it was to help him recover from his injuries as well. He didn't want to strain himself too much and risk getting ill. I looked at the shining knife, it sparkled with the waning light of the day. I watched as the skin wriggled on my arm; something was beneath it. I touched the flat side of the knife against the skin and watched as the worm struggled beneath it. Then I lightly dug the knife into the skin to open it, small droplets of blood dripped out. I caught but a small vision of the worm as it sped back into my body, digging further into the flesh. A sharp, bright, electric feeling went up my arm and struck my neck. I shook my arm, unable to understand what was happening to me. The worm ceased to wriggle in me, I just went into Oliver's trunk and very quietly ripped a piece from a dress of his and tightly wrapped it around the wound, covering it with my sleeve.

Oliver sat up from bed and asked, "What are you doing, Ginny?"

"I… I'm scared Oliver." I breathed, moving to sit next to him.

"What were you doing to yourself?"

"There were these worms…" I cried, feeling desperate. "They won't let me leave the house. You have to do something."

"I can't do anything if the doctor said you must stay in the house." he responded. "But I'll be here for you."

I buried my head in the pillow, feeling my right arm throb from the cut, however I was relieved that the strange wriggling had ended, even if it was only for the moment. "Oliver, what is happening to me?"

"It must be necessary, dear." he answered. "Do you doubt God's purposes?"

"I'm beginning to." I said with a heavy sigh. "They think I'm a lunatic. I don't even hardly know what a lunatic is! A person who has lost their mind? I feel like my mind is the only thing I have... my body is the thing going mad."

"You are the only one who can truly understand it though." Oliver said touching my cheek before he kissed it.

"I don't understand me though!" I cried.

Oliver sat up, his belly rolling just lightly under his ribs and he held his hands together. "You can be patient, though. You can hold on."

"Until what?"

"I don't know the answer to that question, Ginny."

Chapter Twenty

I understood what it meant to be patient and that it was necessary for me to learn to be in this circumstance. For what, until what, and for what purpose, that I didn't know. I told myself I was allowed to be angry this time, as if I was allowed to throw things at the wall and wail at the top of my lungs. And yet I remained silent. I didn't want to give anyone cause enough to put me in a lunatic asylum. All the while I wasted away. I felt weaker and weaker, and everything I ate turned to dust in my mouth, so I didn't eat. My thirst was insatiable, as though nothing I drank could quench it, or even ease it. My body ached and complained as it rotted.

The little worms were back. They crawled throughout my stomach and my arms. I sat near the big window in the bedroom, letting the light fall on my skin, and I took Oliver's knife. Clara and Minnie didn't know I had access to a knife. They didn't look in Oliver's trunk for it. I cut into my flesh, it was no longer smooth and white, but wrinkling and tearing. I saw one of the little worms, curled up in me. I took a pair of tweezers and quickly took a hold of it. It went wild with the touch and started to flail about. I yanked on it, hoping to ease it out of the wound. Part of it was still in me, and so I reached for the candle, and placed the flame near my skin. With fear, it attempted to flee and it let go of my flesh. I finally caught one. I placed it in a jar and watched it move around, as if lost for what to do. It was luminescent, it's whiteness caught the light and reflected it. In reality it was quite pretty, but there were hundreds of them in me, and I couldn't rest until they were out.

I tried to coax all the little worms in my right arm to go to this singular wound, so I didn't need to cut up my entire arm. With the pressure, only a few of them traveled down there, and one after the other, they stopped believing the candle trick and firmly remained, so I had to dig deeper. There were streaks of bright blood lining my arm as I fought to destroy these things. It smelled distinctly like metal. The worms didn't cease moving even when they were outside my body. Dozens of them were in this jar. I thought of adding rubbing alcohol to see what would happen, I thought it'd be cruel though. Yet how cruel was it since they were eating me up? Of course it was their nature to, and their best means of survival, so I was conflicted. How much could a worm think and feel?

Far less than I, I agreed upon. It should be I that I worry about. Was it not the first step to remove them from my body? So I poured a bit of rubbing alcohol from a darkened glass bottle into the bottom of the jar. The worms froze when it hit them. I believed they were either shocked or lifeless now, and most likely the latter. It was a quick death for them. Efficient.

There was a knock on the door, it was Clara. "Ginny? Are you in there?"

"I haven't gone anywhere." I answered, throwing the knife beneath my pillow and pulling down my sleeve. I hid the jar underneath the window sill and covered it with a scarf. She opened the door and stepped in just a bit, her arms crossed.

"What are you doing?" she asked. She was suspicious.

"Looking out the window." I answered. "It is nice outside today. I want to go on a walk."

"Clarence said you're not to leave the house." she replied staunchly. "And there must be good reason for that."

"There is no good reason for keeping me cooped up here." I said.

"It's called confinement for a reason, Ginny."

"It's cruel." I answered.

"If you keep it up, he might just have to keep you on the rest treatment."

"Keeping me in bed would cause nothing but harm, I assure you." I sighed turning around, my eyes welling with hot tears.

"Will you eat?" she asked. "I made food."

"I'm not eating." I responded quickly. "I told you what happens."

"You can't keeping doing this, Ginny! You are going to get even worse if you don't eat!" she cried, her hands straining against one another.

"No, I can't." I answered. "That's true..."

"Ginny... please be reasonable."

"You are the one that doesn't understand. No one... no one understands."

She nodded, her hands nervously feeling the end of her short braid. "That's correct. I don't understand. I don't believe I can understand, but what you're saying is impossible, and thus mad. You need to eat something. Anything. Anything at all."

"I can't. I won't." I said, turning back to the window watching as a cloud went over the sun, making everything an unfortunate gray color. Minnie stepped up to me and put her hand on my shoulder. She felt warm.

"Ginny, if I didn't care, I wouldn't be here, alright? It's important for all of us you get better."

I nodded and said, "I know." I closed my eyes for a moment, seeing the outlines of everything that was bright. She sighed heavily and left me be. I realized that while she was in the room, I didn't feel the worms, but now that I was alone, the worms continued. I pushed my sleeve up again and washed the blood off my arm with a cloth. It looked like I butchered a rat on this window sill. As quietly as I could, I opened the window to let in some fresh air. The breeze was cold but very much welcomed. If I could manage, I'd slip out the window and go running through the field, but there were visions in my mind of me jumping out and landing, breaking both my legs and being stuck there until someone found me, and me too ashamed to cry out for help. So, I didn't. I just dreamed instead, positive dreams. I avoided the nightmares. They were too unpleasant to deal with.

Upon hearing the window open, Opal came running over, a mouse hanging from her mouth. She looked very proud of herself and she jumped up onto the bloody sill, and gave me a look like I was insane. She thought it too, but at least she didn't care. She still purred, and she dropped the mouse on the sill, and it looked like it belonged. She wanted me to eat too. "No, it's yours." I pressed, inching the mouse towards her with my finger tip. The fluffy, brown fur was matted.

Opal lay down and ripped into the mouse to eat it. The crunch was almost unbearable to hear, and yet she was so proud. She was still a relatively plump cat, and her kittens were doing well, wandering around the farm independently. They were doing their job of keeping any other predators away from the chickens, although they were struggling with the hawks and eagles. They could be one of the birds' meals as well if they didn't get away fast enough. That sight I wasn't sure I could deal with, one of my cats hanging from a tree, bloody and ripped to shreds, its fur covering the ground in tufts. A chicken wasn't so bad to see, and there wasn't nearly as much blood. I was used to seeing chickens dead, but not one of my cats.

Too tired to move any longer, I crawled into bed and wrapped myself in the quilts and kept watching Opal. She kept looking at me with soulful, thoughtful eyes. For a moment there, I thought I saw her actually smile. Startled, I buried my head beneath the pillow and blocked out the light.

I woke when Oliver walked through the door after work. "Good afternoon, my dear." I bolted up, shocked by the hour. He chuckled a bit, a smile crossing his face. Last I checked it was around noon. I lost nearly four hours.

"I can't stand being in this room much longer…" I muttered, closing my eyes and stretching out on the bed.

"It'll pass." he said. "As all things do."

"One would only hope that all things do." I said, sitting up quickly, placing my hands on the tops of my bare feet. I traced the hardening lines of veins on my feet. "I miss being free. I just want to go outside and run around in the grass. Might feel something resembling living then."

"And who says you're not free?" he asked with a chuckle.

"Clarence, apparently."

"What if, because of what you see, you are freer than them?" he asked, lightly touching my nose. "You are seeing through the façade, and into what's actually there. Maybe that's what's happening."

"I hope not… God, I hope not. I don't like what I see." I answered. "It's not pleasant, what I'm seeing. I'm seeing death."

"There's a lot of death in this world, Ginny, everything on it dies at some point, and there has been so many hundreds, thousands, of years of people dying all over this planet."

"You sound like Albert." I said, he only chuckled. "But isn't that a little… sad?" My voice cracked.

"Well what do you think happens after we die? Does that sound sad to you?" His eyes were so bright and he was completely at ease. I'm glad he was, because I was far from it.

"For some, yes I'm sure." I answered. "And what is to come is that this world just won't be here anymore."

"As you know it, as you know it. Don't you listen?"

"To Amos? Too much." I answered. He kept smiling, sheepishly, adorably. I rested my head against his chest and he put his hand on my hair.

"You are perfectly capable of weathering this out." Oliver said with a sigh. "You survive. That's what you do."

"Is there an end? Is there any getting better?" I asked, looking into his eyes. They shone right back to me, more colorful than usual. They looked quite glassy, the way glass spit light right back out brighter than it was before. He stood up from the bed and stretched his arms high in the air.

"Now that's up to you."

"I don't understand."

"Didn't say you would."

"You sound suspicious." I quickly added.

He shrugged. "You always used to say that when we were kids."

"That's because it was true." I said with a smile, sitting up on my knees before getting to my feet. "You always used to get me in trouble with mother because I would go outside to play with you and come back and I would be all messy and muddy! She would say that it wasn't lady like to go playing in the dirt."

"And I always said that there was nothing better than dirt to be around." he replied staunchly. "You were the one that would run into the puddles just to jump on them. Somehow most of the splashing landed on my trousers." He kissed my nose and we both giggled. "You wanted to be silly."

"I couldn't be silly if my mother was around." I said.

"That woman…" he sighed, flopping onto the bed. "I don't believe I will understand how someone could grow to become so hard and cold. It was like she was as stiff as a dead body."

"Not my favorite analogy." I said.

"You know what I mean, Ginny. She would never slouch, or even hardly talk. I wonder what her parents were like."

"She was an only child when they made her that way." I answered. "That much I do know. She said they poured so much energy into making her perfect that she wanted to impart the same 'knowledge' onto me." I let out a heavy sigh and started pacing in front of the bed. My ankles felt very restless, like they had to move, and if I wasn't going to walk, I'd just shake my leg until it got too tired to move anymore. That happened a lot. Occasionally I'd kick it against the wall to make it stop. That made too much ruckus though.

"Your grandparents then, what did they do?" he asked.

"Her father worked at the church as the grounds keeper, and grandmother was the secretary." I said. "They weren't wealthy people, but they acted as affluent as they could. Which is odd because no one in these parts is all that wealthy, at least those affiliated at the church. Clara, George and Albert seem to be doing quite well off though, only ones to fit that description."

"They have made a point to." He yawned. "I wish I wasn't so tired. Oh well."

"Agreed. Sometimes I feel like God didn't put a great deal of thought into human beings and how they work. And sometimes it also feels like he threw something together last minute and threw it on the earth… and it just both collapsed and the failure grew to something so wide and uncontrollable that he couldn't do anything about it anymore, or just didn't have the time and energy."

"God not having the energy… that doesn't sound quite right to me." Oliver noted.

"Or he just thought it'd be funny to watch what would happen, and it turned out tragically." I opened up the drawer that I placed the jar of worms in. They were just floating in the solution, and the liquid became a sparkling, luminescent liquid.

"One would think if you place something with a mind and the capabilities a human has, you would probably be aware of things that would come up." Oliver said simply. "And I'm sure God knew what was going to happen. He is God."

"And yet we are taught that man was created blameless." I shook my head and put the jar away. "That's just not be-lievable anymore."

"And why is that when you've been so sure of Amos' teachings?"

"Not all of it, Oliver. How could God put two humans on the earth, man and a woman, and give them hardly a mind, like the mind of a toddler, tell them not to do one thing, and expect them not to do it? I know how a child's brain works."

He chuckled and nodded. "I suppose that could be true."

"And Perry always talks about how God has plans and knows what will happen with all of us and the earth, and that much I can understand, but if that was so, what was the flood and Noah about? Or punishing Adam and Eve for sinning? Or… really anything else that happened."

"Free will." Oliver easily stated.

"How can there be both?" I cried.

"I don't know! I'm not God!" Oliver laughed. "You're asking me too many hard questions."

"You are supposed to help me answer them!" I cried, flopping on the bed beside him. He kissed my belly.

"Once again, I can't! I don't know!" He shook his head. "Ginny, you are going to make yourself mad thinking about this."

"I thought everyone decided I was already there! I have a right then!" I said. If I admitted that I was mad, I shouldn't have been smiling, but I was. Resignation perhaps? Acceptance would be better; however, I wasn't there quite yet. "If I'm mad... then why can't I eat?"

"Because you're mad, not because of anything else, Ginny. Aren't you hungry?"

"Only in the feeling of emptiness in my tummy, nothing else." I said.

"Try eating, and actually eat." Oliver pleaded. "I know Clara and Minnie have been talking to you about it, but will you at least listen to me, though?"

"You don't understand; it isn't food anymore." I stated.

"I do understand. You are mad."

"I'm starting to really dislike that word."

Oliver added, "This marriage thing is difficult."

"Says the sane one." I crossed my arms, and if I was a child, I would have stuck my tongue out at him and run off into the woods somewhere. "Maybe it's worse being sane." I replied quietly. "You have to see me like this."

Chapter Twenty-One

Oliver sat on the edge of the bed, stretching. "We should get out of here." I said, moving to sit behind him, lying my head on his shoulder. "Do you remember when we went swimming?"

"Yes. That pond water was disgusting." he said with a smile, chuckling a bit.

"We should go back there." I stood up and faced him.

He lay on the bed and stared up at the ceiling. "I'm no better at swimming now than I was then."

"You did fine the first time, Oliver!" I exclaimed. "Come on…" I opened the window just enough we could sneak out. It felt so nice to feel the wind on the entirety of my body and my bare feet on the soft, moist ground. Oliver sighed and shook his head, shuffling out of the window. Giggling I pulled him along the road, but he quickly overtook me as if this was a foot race. There was a burst of energy going through me, keeping me steady. My heart was very excitable and adrenaline raced through me. Oliver had a good gait, turning to me with a smile.

"This was your idea Ginny, come on! Keep up!" he called. I tried my hardest to keep up with him. While this explosion of energy was here, I still felt heavier than before this illness had entered me.

"Keep going! Don't wait for me!" I said with a laugh, he turned right towards the pond. I slowed and stared up at the sky, taking in breath, trying to stay standing on my feet. I walked to the pond and was startled to see that Oliver wasn't standing at the edge. Oliver was standing right in the water waving to me, with a calm smile on his face. "You're fast!" I yelled, nearly out of breath. I stood with my feet in the water at the edge of the pond. I slipped my dress off and jumped in the pond, completely wrapped by the chilled water. I swam to him and wrapped my arms around his body and placed my head on his shoulder. "I love you, Oliver." I said.

"I love you too." he said, a smile coming across his face slowly. "We all miss you."

"I miss myself sometimes too." I responded, moving a bit from him, trying to make eye contact as we bounced in the water.

"You'll get better, Ginny, you will." Oliver embraced me again. It had been so long since we were this close. I closed my eyes and relaxed, feeling perfectly at ease. The water enveloped me, leaving me floating in the cold water, without breath. I didn't feel alone… and yet I was. When I opened my eyes all there was, was a kaleidoscope of color intermingling with the daylight fracturing in, holding me. I extended my arms, weightless, comforted. My body was becoming one with earth once again, letting go, returning to its roots. I sunk down, feeling the soft earth beneath me, and there I found a bed, a place to rest. I let out a breath, and went numb.

Immediately there was a heavy wave of water rushing over me, pushing me up over the surface of the pond. Arms went beneath me, pulling me from the water, placing me on the land. The crystalized light became smooth and clear once again, dotted by fluffed clouds and a creamy blue sky. It was Albert hovering over me. "Virginia, Virginia can you hear me?" he asked, I looked into the water for Oliver, but the water reflected the sky. Oliver wasn't there. I tried to reach up but my arm fell limp beside me. "Virginia?"

"Albert?" I choked, a clump of water falling out of my throat. I curled up on my side, staring at the browning, muddy grass. "What... what happened?"

"You're alright." he whispered repeatedly. He picked me up and carried me back to the house. His feet were sure. I was still on this earth. Nature hadn't won.

Once back in my room, alone at last, I cut into my belly, the blood going all the way down to my legs. I'd never looked at myself without clothes on this long in my entire life. I needed relief from the wriggling. These worms had to be removed. I was exhausted fighting them. After a while, I just felt cold and weak, most likely from the blood loss, and I curled up in bed and looked out the window. Something moving caught my eye. There was a deep, dark, grey fog gathering in the distance, rolling over the hills coming towards me. I watched it lethargically. I'd seen things like this for so long that there wasn't anything new to it. They followed every living thing I'd seen.

It ebbed and flowed, moving freely like a living organism as it made its way towards me. Opal looked at it curiously and her hair went up on her back and her tail twitched furiously. She hissed and jumped on the bed away from the bloody sill. The thing started to move like a fish, ducking up and down in the air until it came near the opened window. A right mind would have told me to close the window quickly and run, but I just sat up slightly on my elbow and waited for what was to come. I didn't have enough energy, or cares, to do anything else. I was curious. It slowly poured into the room, and moved along the floor, climbing up the bed. Opal bolted for the closed door. It touched me softly, feeling like cotton, and it wrapped itself around me. I didn't feel fear.

It constricted me, adding pressure like being under-water, until I could no longer take in substantial breath. For a moment I felt like fighting, but my body didn't respond to the trigger in my mind. Instead I just lost everything. It went black.

I woke to a few different things, there was a commotion in the living room, people rustling around and Oliver saying, "Ginny, Ginny, wake up!" He shook my shoulder slightly. I opened my eyes, feeling extremely strange, like there were electric stings all over me. I moved around a bit, trying to get my limbs put together and usable before sitting up and taking in a very deep breath.

"What's going on out there?"

"I don't know, you should look. I need to go to work." He swung his legs over and went out the door and it closed. I stood up, feeling a little shaky. My stomach was growling with hunger. Actual hunger. The feeling was strange, but absolutely pervasive and painful.

In a few moments, I left the room for the living room, but Oliver was already gone. Clara and George were hovering over someone. Albert. He was lying on the couch and was covered in blood and wounds. He was clinging to life. I could see a light floating above him, still connected to his body though. I stood beside the pair who were trying to clean him up. "Where did you find him?"

"On the road outside the house." George said. "We found him on our way here from the store."

Albert's head lolled back and forth and his eyes flickered open. I knelt down beside him and took a hold of his hand. "Hello, Albert." I said calmly. Any enmity I previously held for Albert, vanished. This man was beaten to a pulp shortly after dragging me from the pond. If he had any solid bones in his body, they'd been crushed. "What happened? Can you tell me?" He tried to open his mouth and cried out. "Shh, shh, Albert. I need you to speak."

"It was a group of men..." he said, his voice crackling and gurgling with blood. I pushed him up into a sitting position and placed a cloth in front of him and hit him in the back gently so he coughed up the blood, clearing his lungs and throat. He took in a heavy breath, but there were still bubbles. I bent him further and gently tapped him on the back between the shoulders. A large globular ball of blood plopped out. "From the church." He looked me in the eye. "They blamed me for Oliver's death."

"Oliver's death?" I asked.

"They said I put him in hell."

"He's not dead." I answered, fear leaking into every fiber of my body.

Clara and George looked at one another and they then eyed me. "Virginia," George began. "He's been gone for weeks. He died after the car accident, just about two days after."

I shook my head and stepped back, "No, no, no..." I breathed. "He can't. I've been speaking to him. He's been coming home from work every day!"

My head swirled and ached, and felt like it had hit a wall, and yet the surprise didn't last long. He was magically cured in my mind, just walking in with no injuries when I had seen him near death just a little while before, and he did nothing but go to work and lie in bed to speak with me. There were even nights where I thought I woke and he wasn't there... I just thought he went outside to walk around or something.

I knelt back down and looked to Albert. "I don't blame you for anything that happened with Oliver."

"You should." he said, coughing.

"Not now," I answered. "How about we get you somewhere better to rest." I led him to the daybed against the picture window and brought him a quilt. "And I will get you some clean clothes."

As I went through Oliver's things, his shirts and trousers, his hats and even his few remaining dresses, I questioned if I would speak to Oliver again, now that I knew of his true state. He didn't feel any further away from me now than he did last night when I saw him. He didn't seem dead to me, whatever that entailed. To me, that just meant he was out of a body, and considering the damage done to it, that was probably for the best. As long as I could still speak to him. Still see his face, his eyes, and believe that he was with me...

I found energy in myself, and I wanted to make Albert a cup of hot tea to help soothe his pains. Clara didn't know what to do with me, her reaction to my moving around were actually laughable. As the tea brewed, I took a bite of the bread nearest to us and placed it on my tongue. There was no ash. I swallowed it. Clara's eyes open wide and then with some acid in her breath she said, "Finally."

After giving Albert his tea, I went immediately to the bedroom. I slipped out of my dress and looked at myself in the mirror. I was pale, yes, but it didn't look like death. I didn't feel the worms wriggling inside me trying to get out. I was but a skeleton though. My breasts hung hardly as lumps above stretched skin, and my ribs were prominent. My neck looked like it'd been extended somehow. I touched it and felt how rough the skin was. I was dying. I wasn't dead. My heart raced quickly and there was some urgency in my body, but there was not a dash of hunger left in me. My body gave up on that after so much time. It'd been weeks... I pulled my dress on again, now horribly aware of my appearance.

"I need to eat." I said to Clara.

She nodded with a smile and said, "I've been telling you that for a while. Sit down, sit down. Let me get you something easy to start with. Your body won't be used to this."

"I'm afraid not…" I quietly responded. Albert turned to me and smiled a bit. "Do you feel any better?" He reached out his hand, and the fingers were gently curled up next to his palm. I went and took his hand. "Yes?"

"Oliver was so scared for you." he said. There was a small smile on his face.

"He doesn't need to be." I replied. "Anyways, he has nothing to worry about now."

"In what way?" Clara called. "If we don't fatten you up soon, we'll all have a problem."

George shook his head, almost being amused by his wife's comments. "I'll be fine." I responded, turning to her, straining my neck some, although the energy found but moments ago, drained out of me with the reality of my condition. I sat down beside Albert. "We'll get you all better too."

"All better…" he sighed and shook his head. "There is no such thing."

"You don't believe in a lot of things." I said. "And you know what? I've seen a lot too. Oliver said what I was seeing was real."

He nodded slowly. "We are quite different people."

"We are still people, though. And all people have to face the same realities. You brigaded me about it once. However bad timing it may be, now it's my chance."

He smirked a bit. "Oliver knew you well. I see now…"
"See what?"

"When you visited, you were so timid that I questioned why he would ever trust you. Perhaps my assumptions were wrong."

"Perhaps." I responded, smirking back. I looked him directly in the eye. "You loved Oliver, didn't you?"

He nodded. "If I could love anyone, it was him."

"Why?" I asked, my eyes welling.

"Why? You know him as well as I." Albert looked away, almost as if he was ashamed. "And I knew it would lead to something like this. The people here, they are scared of it. They are afraid of what they can't understand."

"I told Oliver the same once, but everyone around him at one point or another hammered him with a bunch of bible verses." I said. "And what he was taught, everyone else around us was taught the same."

"What you are taught, is nothing more than the continuance of madness." He shook his head. "And fear mongering. There are men out there who will take the same teachings and turn them into campaigns to destroy what people fear. It's dangerous." Albert said quickly before falling into a fit of coughing. I helped him sit up and he wheezed for breath. "And... and... and this... this is what happens." he cried.

"And how did they know about you?" I asked.

"Amos Perry mentioned our friendship to his people, whoever they are." he said, angrily eyeing the window. "He drove Oliver... almost... almost to the brink of... who knows what. I don't know what would have become of Oliver if he stayed here."

"All he saw was... Oliver in a dress." I responded.

"And then comment on it publicly!" Albert cried, wheezing again. "This is what Oliver was afraid of, or this happening to you."

"Now you both need to calm down." Clara said quickly. "It's time for everyone to get something to eat. You don't need to eat any more than you can stomach, but the more the better probably." She eyed both of us. I sat Albert up completely again and we put a tray in front of him. There was some good soup and eggs. Always eggs. One of these days I would decide I hated them probably.

The food actually looked… intimidating. Somehow food could be a scary thing. I went so long without it, and not necessarily by choice, but madness, or whatever curse God thrust upon me, and now I was gifted with the ability to eat again. That meant cooking and digesting, and being hungry. I forgot what hunger really felt like. How could one forget that? It was a primal instinct, but the dead don't feel hunger, and I truly believed I was dead.

"Sally!" I cried, before I even touched the food, realizing my madness could have affected her as well. Fear drained me, as well as sickness for what reality most likely held.

"She's alive." Clara said simply, not even looking at me.

"And… I've thought she's been dead." I responded quickly.

Clara shook her head. "I'm aware. She's with Minnie right now. She's been primarily under her care."

My heart beat quickly and there was an aching acid seeping through me. I hit my head against the table, trying to fathom what could have been so wrong with me that I neglected my own daughter. "How… how could I?" I cried. I surely wasn't hungry now and I leaned back away from the table and stared ahead blankly, my eyes welling with tears. How could I not notice? Yet I never saw her move. She just laid there, silent, decomposing, being carried around limply by the others in the house. She never approached me, spoke to me… but she must have. She was such a talkative girl. She was so smart… and I missed it, so much time. So much learning…

"You need to eat now, Virginia. We will worry about Sally in a bit." Clara said gruffly, almost annoyed. I bit into the apple, feeling the juice cover my mouth with the sweet taste. It was enjoyable actually. I ate it, and felt how empty my stomach was, and smeared some jam on a roll and ate that as well. I closed my eyes and tried to listen to my body, my real body. It didn't tell me to stop so I went with some eggs. The taste was so familiar, and almost negatively so, and yet I ate. "How are you, sad little people doing?" Clara asked laughing after about an hour of eating. We both glared at her.

Albert stood up, annoyed and got on his feet, but he shook a bit and looked like he was going to fall. "It is not safe for you to go, Albert." George said quickly. "Albert…"

"I should get back to my house." Albert responded.

"And how do you plan to do that?" George asked. "Your car is outside of the church, half destroyed. Do you plan to walk there and just leave without issue?"

Albert sighed and upon realizing the difficulty of doing so, stopped. If not deflated before, he was now. His eyes were angry and tired. His face just sagged with exhaustion. "In what world, would your God have an issue with me?"

"Because you said your God." I responded. I received a glare.

"And what makes you think that he's mine?" he asked. "You said so yourself that they use language, literature sup- posedly from God, against people like me."

"I know." I sat down, my legs started to shake. I tried to ignore it best I could.

"And do you think there is any hope for me?"

"I have to." I answered honestly. "Because Oliver is like you."

"Was." he added quietly.

The word was hit me with some force. It hurt. "Yes, but did you not hear me?"

"I heard you."

"Finish your food." Clara said. "And both of you need to stop acting like you need to go back to Dr. Goldman."

Chapter Twenty-Two

Albert was weak, understandably, his mobility was lessened and we wanted to stay in the farmhouse until he recovered enough to go with George and retrieve his car to go home. He could hardly walk a couple of feet without either becoming incredibly frustrated in which case he started shouting, or collapsing. He'd tense up so badly that all of his muscles would cramp and he'd get all swollen. He wasn't very good at taking care of himself. Not that I had much to say about the subject, I was a failure in that department.

That night when I walked in my bedroom alone, and Oliver had never returned from work, I felt like he was gone. That he truly wasn't going to be lying next to me at night. There was a confusing feeling of complete emptiness, and yet safety. He was gone. That was true. And being a widow at 24 was not something I ever considered. He couldn't comfort me or encourage me any longer, and his voice would soon fade from my memory. And yet he was watching from above or beside, something. He was with me.

I sat on the bed and stared ahead, deciding what emotion it was I felt. Then Sally burst in the door and jumped on me, and hugged me. "Mama!" she cried. I held her and kissed her cheek, so happy to feel her alive and well. "Papa says goodbye." she said to me. "I saw him outside."

"You did?" I asked, smiling sadly. She nodded. "That was very nice of him."

"Can we go see him tomorrow?" she asked.

"I suppose we can." I responded.

"How come you can see me now?" she asked, lying down on my bed.

"I don't know." I said tiredly, kissing her cheek. "But I'm glad I can." I lifted her up in my hands. Her skin was soft and supple now. There was so much light in her eyes. Her voice had grown, and I appreciated hearing it. "You're such a pretty girl." I said, touching her curls.

"You're pretty too Mama." she said.

If I could manage to convince Clarence to allow me to leave the house, I would be finished with this confinement, and as angry as it the process made me, he believed it worked. I knew confinement was wrong. Before that spirit approached me, I was cutting myself open to pull out worms.

The next morning, Clarence was across the table from me at breakfast, and I was eating. Minnie uncomfortably sat between us, while Albert was still asleep in the day room. "You think you want to leave?" Clarence asked.

"I want to go see Oliver's grave." I said, hating all the words that just came out of my mouth.

He sighed and looked at Minnie. "Do you think she is well enough?"

Minnie nodded. "If I didn't think so, I wouldn't have asked you to come, Clarence." There was some heat in her voice. Through this all, she stood by me. Last night, Clara talked to her in some detail about the progress I was making. If one could say that it was progress at all, but if I told Clarence that, he'd think I was still mad.

"We may need to see Dr. Goldman first, to determine if she can leave her confinement."

"Isn't going to the doctor, leaving?" I asked. "Clarence, I'm not asking for much. I just want to see where Oliver is."

Clarence took in a deep breath. "I suppose we may go."

"Albert should come with us." I suddenly added.

Clarence looked shocked, just as shocked as he was that Albert was in this house at all. "You must be joking, Virginia." He placed his head in his hands and closed his eyes.

"No, I'm not." I stated solidly. "I would appreciate it if you took me seriously for once."

Clarence shook his head and said, "I've never tried to be difficult with you, Virginia. You're my sister. You are my responsibility to take care of properly, especially now that your husband cannot."

"You make it sound like I'm a burden." I said, putting the toast back down on the plate.

"At times, people can be burdens." Clarence noted, avoiding eye contact.

"I want to go, and Albert should come with us." I said again, a bit harder. Clarence's eyes expressed sadness, and weight. He continued to avoid eye contact. "And I want you to tell me who did this to Albert. I know you know."

He took in a deep breath. "The same people who did this to you."

Minnie looked at him with shocked eyes. "What are you talking about Clarence?" she cried in fear.

Resigned he added, "Reverend Perry was preaching about how we need to hate evil and how it must be purged from the earth. They considered Oliver to be evil, and so they took advantage of an opportunity when they saw it. When they saw him in the automobile, they... they struck." He took a breath. My heart beat with anger and the same hate they must have felt for my husband. "And upon his death, and Virginia's illness, they thought God was striking her with some curse because of her husband's sins, and so they went after the cause of those sins, and ended up with Albert."

"And you think I'm mad." I muttered. "Reverend Perry caused my husband's death? Does he not understand 'thou shall not kill?' does he not understand he can't just kill whoever he likes in the name of God!" I was shouting now, my face filled with heat and blood.

Clarence stood up as well, although he was far calmer than I. "Yes, he does believe he can do that, and who are the rest of us to disagree?"

"Do you not have a working mind of your own? The ability to make decisions? The sense of what is good and what is bad with your own actions?" I asked.

"They saw it as a responsibility." Clarence added, his voice hardly audible. He crossed his arms.

"They must not be able to see the difference in their own actions. Self-righteous hypocrites, all of them. You too!" I accused.

"Me?" he asked, shocked.

"You believe them, don't you?" I asked.

He took in a deep breath and looked away. "You don't understand Virginia."

"What don't I understand? The fear? The coercion? I lived it too Clarence. And this is where it put me."

"Let's go to the cemetery." he said quietly. "Let's just go."

"Thank you." I pressed. "I'll get Albert." I went to the day room where he was resting. My yelling must have woken him. He sat up, grasping the quilt in his hands. Sally was fast asleep next to him, her little arms stretched right above her, and a bit of drool dried on her cheek. Albert laughed when he saw her.

"Beautiful daughter you have there." Albert said.

"I know." I said with a laugh. "Thank you. Do you think you can get put together here soon? We are going to see Oliver."

"His grave." he corrected.

"Yes, that." I said, slightly annoyed with his tone, but otherwise resigned. Albert stood up, wobbly on his feet, grasping the daybed he had been situated on for a few days now. Sally groggily woke up and looked at us. She swept her hair aside and yawned. "Come on Sally, go get your coat." I said, patting her shoulder.

"We going to see Papa?" she asked.

"Yes."

"Why? He's not there." She looked at me, utterly confused. For a moment I was silent, attempting to formulate an answer. "He's in heaven you know." I smiled a bit and nodded. "He said it's very nice there. Said it's warm."

"We can go give him flowers at least." I responded, patting her head. "Would you go gather them up quickly, Sally?"

She nodded and ran off, her little legs looking unsteady. On went her coat, and to the garden she flew. I smiled, watching, hoping that she would safely go through life, her father able to watch her from above. Albert shook his head smiling. "The honesty of a child." he said.

"Honesty? Possibly awareness." I said. "She had nothing blocking her from this side to the other." I sat down beside him as he tried to pull his boots on.

"Awful to think about." he said.

"What? That there are things you don't actually know?" I said with a laugh.

He nodded slowly and strained to pull the laces tight. "Exactly. As an academic I've strived for knowledge, for the truth, but truth doesn't exist."

"Maybe it doesn't." I said. "That's not our job to know."

"I'm still so curious. That doesn't take the curiosity away."

The cemetery was inside of the city, near the Catholic church. There were two sides to the cemetery, one for Catholics, nearest to the church, and one for Protestants, on supposedly, less sanctified ground. There was a large heavy gate standing before the land with a bell in a tower. It was rung immediately before any burial was to take place. Directly inside was a large carved stone cross and beyond that, the place was dotted with a variety of headstones. I avoided walking on these grounds most of my life for fear that I walked on the dead, but I had cause to be here now. Sally held my hand and was tightly grasping a bouquet of flowers. Minnie led us to the grave which was nothing extraordinary, just a simple limestone brick that said: Oliver Crain, born July 15th 1895, died May 29th 1922, aged 27 years. The stone was long, there was room for my name to go on there, as well as Sally's if she so chose. Sally put the flowers down in front of the stone and then she kissed the letters before taking a hold of my skirt. I smiled a bit and waved.

Albert was blinking really fast, trying to keep away tears. He then knelt down and began to weep before the grave. I knelt beside him and placed my hand on his back, and laid my head on his shoulder. Sally too hugged him. Albert smiled when she came near and then she sat on his lap and hugged him. He calmed some. "You know where Papa is." Sally said. "Don't be sad."

About the Author

Nina Wilson is a graduate of Coe College in Cedar Rapids Iowa. She lives in Indianola Iowa with her family. She loves history, especially early English history, photography, traveling, fishing, and camping. Her novel *Surrender Language* was published by Adelaide Books in 2017. *Malady* is her second published novel.

www.ingramcontent.com/pod-product-compliance
Lightning Source LLC
Chambersburg PA
CBHW020400030726
47496CB00007B/2239